I0557635

A Heart in Port

by

Cate Masters

Christmas in the Castle

This is a work of fiction. Names, characters, places, and incidents are either the product of the author's imagination or are used fictitiously, and any resemblance to actual persons living or dead, business establishments, events, or locales, is entirely coincidental.

A Heart in Port

COPYRIGHT © 2023 by Cate Masters

All rights reserved. No part of this book may be used or reproduced in any manner whatsoever without written permission of the author or The Wild Rose Press, Inc. except in the case of brief quotations embodied in critical articles or reviews.
Contact Information: info@thewildrosepress.com

Cover Art by *Rae Monet, Inc.*

The Wild Rose Press, Inc.
PO Box 708
Adams Basin, NY 14410-0708
Visit us at www.thewildrosepress.com

Publishing History
First Edition, 2023
Trade Paperback ISBN 978-1-5092-5229-9
Digital ISBN 978-1-5092-5230-5

Published in the United States of America

The image of grace, Maddie did her best to appear comfortable and pleasant while Zack climbed into his place beside her. What a terrible impression she must have made on the poor man when first they met.

And now her father was intent on putting them both in a poor light. She would have to counter his efforts.

Luckily, Zack appeared not to notice any subterfuge as he conducted the tour of the estate. With utmost good nature, he pointed out various areas and went on about the plan of the landscape designer, Frederick Olmsted.

For nearly everything Zack told them, Father had a question. Maddie knew what he was doing—trying to figure out the man's scam. Everyone worked a scam, whether big or small. Her father had taught her that early. The knowledge saved her from making a few huge mistakes in her life. No one deserved trust, he said, and she still found it difficult to give it away.

But was that true even of someone with genuine charm, like Zack? She made a point of studying him as he spoke with her father. No matter how Papa phrased his questions, Zack answered with cheerful enthusiasm. The more genuine Zack was, the more intent her father grew. She could almost hear the inner workings of his brain, trying to figure out the man's game. What her father didn't seem to fathom was the possibility there was no game. Just refreshing honesty.

Praise for Cate Masters

Reviewers have praised Cate's other stories:

"Even though the book is short, Ms. Masters packs a punch in the depth of her characters, the emotional dialogue between the characters and the pacing is great not rushed. And the ending... *sigh*"

~Harlie's Reviews

"Now this is my kind of short story, or any [kind of] story to be fair. It had me hooked from the first word."

~BTSE Magazine

"Cate Masters is able to tell a story with engaging characters, romance, and a strong heroine—no shrinking violets here! It is a magnificent escape from reality."

~Ruth, My Devotional Thoughts

"Sweet, romantic and exciting, I read this book in one sitting as I couldn't put it down."

~All Romance

"Cate can really tell a tale."

~Ramblings of a Book Lunatic

"This story is worth the read!"

~The Romance Studio

Dedication

To Gary,
who has always been my heart in port

Chapter One

Amid the rock and rattle of the train, the sparkle of morning frost in the landscape passing outside caught Madelyn Winterborn's eye. She closed her book, pressed close to the window, and breathed in the crisp October air. Another holiday season would soon be upon them. Another disappointment.

Her breath fogged the glass. Through the mist, vague shapes began to form. She could almost see two figures, hand in hand, before a large fir tree. She startled at the sound of her mother whispering, *Maddie...*

Mama...?

"I haven't seen that in a long time."

At her father's voice, the daydream melted like the frost beneath the rising sun. Alfred Winterborn was not one to comment on trivialities. It must be something truly unusual.

Setting aside disappointment at the interruption, Maddie shifted to see the spectacle. A thud, and her heart fell, along with the book she'd held. She retrieved the precious memento from the floor. Her place in the pages lost, she brushed away grime from the lettering of the title, *Poems* by Emily Dickinson. One of her mother's prized possessions. One of the few things of Mama's that Father hadn't sold.

With a firm hold on the book, she turned to him. "What was it?"

1

"A smile." Her father leaned closer. "Yours."

He'd caught her, heart on sleeve. Something he'd taught her never to do. Sentimentality was a luxury. She lifted her chin in the manner of a haughty heiress. Something else he'd taught her, though it couldn't have been further from the truth.

"Looking forward to seeing the castle?"

"It's not a true castle."

"Don't speak like that," he hissed. "Even in private." Gone was the whimsical tone, though it had taken longer than usual for his temper to flare. "Mr. Vanderbilt has gone to great expense. Dedicated the last five years to constructing a fine estate. Talk like that would ruin our chances. I'm risking too much for my business as it is, by undertaking this deal…"

His voice faded from her head, and mixed with the whoosh and clack of the train. The sigh in her breast stayed there, though she nearly burst with the effort. When would he stop treating her like a student? And not even his star pupil, but one who required constant pestering, cajoling, repetition. She knew the rules all too well.

What would her life have been like, had Mama not died? She could have been a real student, in a cozy classroom, with friends for schoolmates. Papa could have come home from his job and been content to live in their home, the same home she'd known since birth. True, he was never thrilled with his work, but he was so clever at business, and shrewd with numbers.

All he did now was manipulate figures at the expense of others, which necessitated a life on the road, never staying too long in one city. Hence, their rushed trip to provide medieval adornments to a castle in North

Carolina, of all places.

From the center of her jumbled thoughts came her mother's voice again: *Princes will favor you, but a kingly love will heal your heart on Christmas.*

A repeat of some of the last words her mother had spoken. At the time, Maddie thought Mama must have been delirious. Though her words sustained Maddie in dark times and gave her hope for happiness someday, none of it made sense. How could it? They had no dealings with royalty. Except this business that awaited in Asheville made it seem as if they did.

Her father's drone rose above the noise again. Maddie had the strange sensation the train was barreling into the unknown and yet frozen in time. Which oddly made sense, since she'd lived and relived this same moment with her father, always just before a new job. This one was different. This outcome, said a niggling sensation, would be like no other.

The thought sent a shiver over her, and she rubbed her arms and squeezed her eyes shut.

"Madelyn! Are you listening?" he hissed.

"Pardon?" Even as she spoke, she heard the word's hollow ring. She shook off the strange feeling. Straightening her shoulders, she sat taller. "Yes, Father. Sorry. I'm a bit travel-weary."

"Buck up, my girl. You must be at your best."

Yet her best was never good enough, was it? "I always am, Father." When would he realize it? Always, the job came first. Others would describe their enterprise less as business risk than as scam. The very reason Maddie hadn't seen England since her girlhood, their homeland where actual castles had been built centuries ago. The place where disaster was rooted, yet its

3

tentacles reached for her still.

He patted her wrist. "This Christmas will be special."

"Will it?" Maddie doubted it. Christmas hadn't been special since they'd lost Mama.

"Very special," he went on. "Like it used to be." He squeezed her shoulder.

Her heart likewise squeezed. A glimmer of hope kindled inside her. "Do you mean it, Papa?"

"You'll see. Our best yet." He winked.

She set a smile on her lips, weak enough to hold without break, strong enough, she hoped, to appear true. At least, true enough to stop his tired old spiel. "Of course, Father." As if he didn't repeat the same promise every year. And fail to keep it.

Yet something about the way he spoke made her think he actually believed it.

When he opened his mouth to continue, she gave an exaggerated sigh. "How much longer until we reach Asheville?"

She hardly bothered to listen to his detailed recount of the route.

"From there, we'll take a carriage to the estate," he finished.

"They're expecting us?"

"I'm meeting Mr. Vanderbilt tomorrow afternoon." He sank deeper into the plush seat. "Mr. George Washington Vanderbilt."

Maddie side-eyed him. Was he practicing the awestruck act, or had Vanderbilt truly inspired it? Or did his scheme this time include pawning her off to the millionaire? To forge a gravy train to last a lifetime?

She shook off the notion. Not even her foolhardy

parent would go that far. Would he? The mountains were breathtaking, but she had no wish to live in a castle. And especially not with some stuffy tycoon.

Her father went silent and eventually tilted his hat over his eyes. Only then did she relax and return to her book. Next she knew, the train was pulling into the station. With a snort, her father startled awake, his tight smile an acknowledgement and an unspoken prompt to get ready.

On cue, Maddie put on her best expression, straightened her spine, and smoothed her dress. Others shuffled along the aisle.

With graceful precision, she stepped out behind her father, mindful of the glances and outright stares. She'd been told she was pretty, even beautiful. When needed, she could pass for much younger than her twenty years. Tools, her father taught her, that were extremely useful for them both. She provided a distraction so he could conduct his business without an overly watchful eye on him.

She never quite worked out how such skills were useful to her, but her mother would have wanted her to aid her father however needed. Wouldn't she?

A blast of cold hit her face when she stepped down, and she steadied her hat with one hand. People bustled past and complained of the frigid temperature. Maddie had endured worse, at home in England. And much better, in Jamaica.

But she couldn't think of either place right now. Her father was already headed in the direction of a man and wagon. *A wagon?* That couldn't be right. They'd expected a carriage.

But Papa briskly shook the man's hand, and after a

brief exchange, the driver loaded their two bags in the back.

A sharp glance from her father made her realize she'd dallied. Somehow she held her pleasant expression on her hurried approach.

"Ah, finally. My daughter Madelyn." Papa extended an arm as if to pull her into an embrace.

"Miss." The man touched his cap. "So just the two of you?"

"Yes." Her father strained to look at something behind her. "Pardon. I'll be right back."

Alarmed, Maddie tracked his hasty departure across the dirt roadway, where he shook hands with yet someone else. This man, with collar raised and hat brim low, looked much less friendly.

"Will he be very long?" asked the driver.

Maddie tried to think of some plausible excuse and turned to respond, but all that came out when she turned to him was, "Oh!"

The man raised his brows and seemed to suppress a grin.

"Excuse me." *Get hold of yourself, Maddie.* "I didn't realize…I mean, I thought you…" Heat flushed up her neck to her cheeks. She could barely look at his youthful face. A face so handsome, shockwaves went through her.

"Is something wrong?" He sounded amused.

Which inflamed her anger. She lowered her chin and batted her eyes. "Not at all. I assumed you were older." And less attractive. Much less attractive.

"If you're worried, let me assure you of your complete safety."

His gaze wandered over her face as he spoke, causing her to cast doubt on that assertion.

Her skin prickled. "Is that so?" She pinned him with a glare. When his face reddened, she felt the tide turn in her favor.

"I grew up here," he assured her. "I know every road from here to Biltmore Estate."

Estate. Just as she'd thought. "Father told me it was a castle?"

Another smile, somewhat embarrassed. "Yes. Well, not yet, but it will be. It's nearly complete." He inclined his head across the street. "Will your father be much longer?"

She'd nearly forgotten. A glance reassured her. "Here he comes." A closer look stole her confidence. He wouldn't meet her gaze. He had that casual air about him, the one he purposely wore for strangers.

"Change of plan," Papa said to the driver. "You take Madelyn, and I'll be along later."

"Papa, no."

"Darling, yes." Still averting his gaze, he spoke in his no-nonsense voice and gave the driver a pleasant, but expectant, smile.

The man glanced from him to her. "Sir, I was told to fetch you both."

"And so you have. My bag, at least. And my daughter."

A sourness filled her mouth. How kind of him to mention her, after his bag.

The driver gave an incredulous laugh. "The estate is nearly an hour away, and some of the roads are—"

Father's smile turned to steel. "I will find my way. After I conclude some business."

Dumbstruck, panic rose in Maddie. "Father," she nearly hissed through her gritted teeth, stuck in a smile.

An icy glare, and he squeezed her hand a little too hard. "You'll be fine. Mr. Kingley will deliver you to the castle."

She shook her head. *There's no castle.* This was all wrong.

He dropped her hand and left without another word.

She could only stare after him. The book she held helped to ground her, as if she held her mother's hand.

"Miss? I hate to rush you, but we really should be going." He extended a hand to help her into the wagon, but she barely touched it, and settled on the wooden bench. The very uncomfortable, cold wooden bench.

He said something, and pulled a blanket from behind the seat. "So you don't catch a chill."

She accepted it with a nod. She'd already caught more than a chill. She'd been frozen out. What was her father up to? She wasn't actually sure what she was supposed to be telling anyone about their visit, her father's business deal, or any of it.

The blanket scratched her cheek, but she pulled it tight around her and, still clutching her book, focused on the road ahead. The less she revealed to this man or anyone, the better.

****

Alarm radiated from the girl seated beside Zack. She might have been a china doll on a shelf instead of a girl in a wagon. After one backward glance, she snapped forward and pulled the blanket so tight she looked like she wanted to disappear inside it.

And who could blame her? He could only imagine her discomfort. Here she was, passed off to a total stranger, headed down a lonely stretch of road as the town fell away behind them. What sort of father did that to his daughter?

"Is this your first time in Asheville?" Stupid question. He'd have remembered her if she'd visited before. Those auburn locks and deep brown eyes caught him quicker than quicksand.

"Yes." She turned her head away but flicked her gaze in his direction.

Probably just anxious. He felt it his duty to put her at ease. "Where do you hail from?"

"England." She hunkered deeper inside the blanket.

"Your accent sort of gave that away." He chuckled. "We weren't properly introduced. I'm Zack Kingley."

Her only response was a nod. And a stiff one at that. Okay, he would keep the conversation going. "And you're Madelyn Winterborn." He expected another nod, at least, but none came.

"I doubt we'll see much of each other during your stay." Stupid thing to say. "I'm mainly in charge of the grounds." Still no reaction. "I understand your father will be providing some fine items from English castles? Tapestries and suits of armor and such?"

"I suppose."

He made a noise of acknowledgement. Her father must not keep her informed of details. "Those will really fit the vision Mr. Vanderbilt has for Biltmore. He had it designed like your old castles."

He practically sensed her eyeroll. Of course, not *her* castles. Why did he say that?

Tugs at the blanket turned to an apparent wrestling match, with the blanket winning. The girl twisted in her seat, then got to her feet and leaned over.

"No, please don't—" He reached for her.

A rut in the road jolted the wagon upward. Her hand

shot to the rail. Some small object sailed over the side.

"Oh!" Too fast, she bent to catch it.

He jerked back the reins. The horse snorted, tossed its head. The wagon lurched to a halt.

The girl tumbled out with the tiniest squeal.

"Miss!" He scrambled after her and caught sight of her blue dress disappearing down the embankment. Toward the stream.

"Blazes!" Following her path, he dug his boots into the ground, cursing again when he slipped on loose dirt and wet leaves. *What is she doing?*

On all fours at the edge of the stream, she reached a hand toward the lost object. *A book?*

"Wait," he called. "The ice is too thin. Don't lean on—" A crack like a whip split the air. Then a splash as she plunged head first into the frigid waters. In one hand, she held the book aloft while she struggled to free herself from the current.

He plunged one boot beside her in the stream. Frozen water shocked his breath from him for a moment, and then he swept her up in his arms. Cold seeped into his jeans from her wet dress. "We had an early freeze. Very unusual for Asheville." Why was he telling her this? Her teeth chattered, but she gave no response.

He held her trembling body against his, but the steep embankment hindered his climb. "Can you walk?"

"Yes." Still clearly dazed, she stretched her boots without hesitation to the ground.

"Slow and easy." He used his body to shield her from a fall. Step by faltering step, they made their way to the road.

The horse nickered. "Good Goliath." Extra carrots later for the Clydesdale for its patience.

"Goliath?" she asked through chattering teeth.

He lifted her up into the wagon. Light as goose down, she was. "Because he's a giant. A gentle giant, but never let him step on your feet with those oversized hooves."

"I'll try to remember that." Distress filled her face as she examined the book. "What is it you expect as payment? I have to warn you, we are not in any position at the moment to—"

"That." He let himself take in her expression of mistrust, guarded apprehension, that gave way to some confusion. The softening was what made it all worthwhile.

"What?"

He couldn't hold back a chuckle. "I want nothing, really. It just makes me feel good to help someone in need." And her especially.

To move past the subject, he fluttered the blanket open and tucked her in, then ran to the driver's seat. Each step sent sharp prickles through his foot and ankle. She likely suffered worse, he told himself, and took up the reins. "I'll have you there in two shakes of a lamb's tail."

She sent him a small but perfect smile. "My mother used to say the same thing."

"As did mine." Why that should give him a warm feeling, he couldn't say, but returned her smile with genuine pleasure. A flick of his wrist sent Goliath forward, and two clicks of his teeth hurried the pace.

Conversation forgotten, he concentrated on keeping Goliath at an even trot. The castle loomed in the distance like something from another time. Sometimes he imagined knights on stallions, feathers decorating the headdresses of both. Nonsense, his father would say. But without his imagination, how could he envision the plans for a new landscape? "Nearly there."

The long road that led to the entrance shrank with the steady clop of hooves, too slow for Zack's liking. If he was cold, the girl must be freezing. He wasted no time getting her inside.

Mrs. Elliott swept a critical gaze over her, but directed him to an empty bedroom. "Where's Mr. Winterborn?"

"He'll be along directly." Zack had no inclination to explain or gossip. Ignoring the head housekeeper's dismay, he set the girl on a cushioned chair and told her, "I'll fetch your bag so you can change into something dry."

Mrs. Elliott followed him into the hall. "I'll ask Mrs. Sullivan for some tea."

He gave a nod of thanks and headed outside. He shouldn't have left the wagon out front, but surely Mr. Vanderbilt would excuse it this once. Madelyn's suitcase, tucked behind the seat and next to the feed bags, struck him as overly light for such a long journey. He tried not to wonder about its contents on the way back to her room.

Outside her door, he knocked and waited.

After a moment came a soft, "Who is it?"

"Zack." No response. "The driver, miss. I have your bag."

"One moment, please." A click, and the door opened a crack. One large brown eye scanned his length.

He raised the bag into view. "Shall I set it out here?" The last thing he wanted to do was cause her further anxiety.

"Thank you."

"Would you mind," he asked as he placed it in the doorway, "if I came back later to see how you're doing?"

Another hesitation, and her demeanor changed, as if she threw off her shyness and put on an invisible suit of armor. "That would be fine."

"Very good." He winked, which seemed to take a small chink out of her armor. A challenge he considered worthwhile to discover the girl beneath these layers of protection. From what, he wondered?

Throughout the afternoon, he tried to steer his thoughts to work, but they always circled back to the girl. Madelyn Winterborn. Was there a lovelier name? Or a lovelier girl?

Her dark hair set off her little rosebud mouth and fair skin. It wasn't just her almond-shaped eyes that struck him, but that they were filled with such depth. He wanted to explore that depth. Hear her stories of travel and adventure. And sorrow. He was certain there were sad tales among them.

Something about her compelled him to return. To make sure she had all that she needed. If he could make her smile, his efforts would be rewarded.

Duties kept him busy until after dinner. He hesitated to intrude on her privacy. Maybe she was already asleep, exhausted from her journey.

One quick visit. Then he'd leave her in peace.

When he stood outside her room, his nerves rattled. Light shone from beneath the door, but the fireplace would be lit. No noise came from inside. Should he leave?

Then he heard the clink of china. She was awake after all.

One knock, and he readied to go.

"I'm coming."

Two little words sent a buzz through his chest. One that spread through his body when she filled his vision.

Her long hair was swept to one side. Rather than bleary, her eyes were bright and warm. "So you came back after all."

She'd been waiting? "As promised."

"Come in, then." She gestured to the fireplace, where two chairs faced one another.

"You're looking well. I'm glad the trip didn't wear you out." He waited for her to sit before taking the seat opposite.

"Not at all."

From that, he sensed she'd endured much worse. "Glad to hear it. Mrs. Sullivan sent a dinner tray, I see. She's a wonderful cook."

"Indeed." Back straight as a board, she folded her hands in front of her.

Still not feeling talkative. No matter. He could fill in the gaps. "Did your father arrive safely?"

"Not yet."

"Oh." A vague sense of alarm swept over him. Mr. Winterborn was a grown man capable of taking care of himself. He should have more concern for his daughter, though.

"I'm sure he'll be along soon."

"Yes, I'm sure."

Her brows twitched, then her mouth. Then she burst into a smile. A glorious, full smile.

"What?" Had he missed something?

"You have...a bit of dirt. Just there." She pointed to her cheek.

Oh, no. He brushed his fingers over his face. "Sorry.

I washed up, but missed—"

"Please don't bother. It's rather charming."

He couldn't tell if she teased him or flirted with him. Finally, he gave in and smiled. "It's been a day."

"So it has."

One he had no regrets about. In fact, this was the best ending to a work day he could remember. He could sit with her a long time, just staring into her eyes.

But the silence was stretching too long. He broke the awkward moment. "Is there anything else I can get you?"

He might as well have thrown cold water over her again. Her expression blanched, and she stood. "Nothing, no."

"I should let you get some rest."

"I'm not tired. I thought you meant…" She clasped her hands.

He held back the urge to take her hands in his, warm them like she warmed his heart. "I'm in no rush. Unless you want to be alone."

"No."

The way she said it so fast made him think she'd spent too many nights on her own.

Her breathy laugh gave away her embarrassment. "I was only going to read."

He stepped back to the chair and sat. "I'd love some poetry."

"You would?"

He wished she'd sit again. "Very much."

"I only have the one volume."

"I think your book may be dry. Or nearly." He retrieved it from a rack beside the fire. "Emily Dickinson. A popular poet, I've heard. But I could have just bought you a new copy." His shelves were filled with text books, history, and biographies. Poetry would be a rare treat. He hoped.

"Nothing can replace this. My mother gave it to me." She cradled it against her and finally sat.

When she began to read, he was swept away. She might have written the words herself. Each poem gave away her longings and fears and hopes (the thing with feathers—he liked that). And her convictions. She recited, "Tell all the truth, but tell it slant," as if it was her personal motto.

After a few pages, her cadence slowed, and she held a hand to her mouth and yawned. "Sorry."

"You're tired. Why not climb into bed, and I'll read to you?" He quickly added, "From this chair. I won't move."

She finished for him, "And you're a man of your word."

"I am." So she had paid attention.

"Very well." She handed him the book as she passed.

He averted his gaze while she climbed beneath the covers. It seemed the gentlemanly thing to do. When she settled, he began.

The lines soon ensnared him. Simple scenes from life, like a bird on a walk, and feeling like a nobody. But the others threw open a doorway to the unknown. A funeral in her brain?

The girl had depths, all right. Darkness and depth. He wanted to shine a light on every layer. Keep her warm. Let her know that death's carriage would not stop for her, not while he was near.

The last one he read a few times. Wild nights. Yes, he could imagine the two of them, him rowing a little boat in Eden. And mooring in one another. The poem sent him into a dream state where he happily stayed.

****

"What's going on here?" a loud someone demanded.

Maddie startled awake. "Papa. You're here." Finally.

"I'm not the only one." He gave a pointedly stern look to the person in the chair.

The young man hunched forward and pressed his fingers to his eyes. "I must've dozed off."

"Why are you in my daughter's room?" Father ignored the man's look of confusion. "Are you trying to take advantage of her?"

Pleasantness hardened to sternness. "Certainly not."

How absurd. "Papa, he was very kind—"

"Quiet, Maddie. I will deal with you later."

Oh, no. Not this time. "There is nothing to deal with. He saved me from the stream." Her father's head inclined like a question mark, so she went on. "After I fell from the wagon." She bit her lip. Oh, why had she revealed such a thing?

In a dramatic spasm, Papa tossed his head and flailed his arms at Zack. "What? You put my only child in mortal danger?"

"Oh, hardly, Papa."

He turned on her. "Quiet!" Then back to him. "I assure you, Mr. Vanderbilt will hear about this."

She threw her legs over the side of the bed. Her father wasn't going to try to shake down the driver, was he? "It was an accident."

Father pointed at her. "I'm warning you, Maddie. Stay out of this."

There was only one way to stop him. Laughter. "Out

of my own clumsiness? Really, Father. That's all it was. No one's fault but my own." Beneath her cavalier exterior, she met his glare with her own.

Her father looked down his nose at her. "We will speak more of this in the morning. When you're thinking more clearly." With that, he spun on his heel and was down the hall.

"Thank you for that." Zack rose. "I'm glad you're feeling better. I really should leave now. Here's your book. I enjoyed the poems."

Her heart filled with a fuzziness, a floating feeling she hadn't experienced in too long. Despite his misgivings, he'd saved the book for her.

"Do you fancy other books?"

She ran her fingers across the cover. "So many. I love to read."

"So does Mr. Vanderbilt. He has a very extensive library. Perhaps he'll lend you others while you're here."

She studied Zack. "Don't worry about Father. He's overly protective." She wished. A protective father would never have abandoned her.

From his expression, Zack was thinking the same thing.

His disappointment seemed aimed at himself. "I should have protected you from harm."

"I rely only on myself for protection." Since she was a girl. Since Mother died, she'd had to.

"Well, then." The rigid set of his smile hinted at frustration. "Maybe you can return the favor sometime."

To be in another's debt made Maddie uncomfortable. People tried to call in favors at the worst time, her father always said. She didn't want that sort of obligation hanging over her.

"Thank you again."

A curt nod, and he stepped to the door frame. "Rest well."

"You, too." The urge to ask if she'd see him in the morning nearly won out over level-headed restraint. Of course she'd see him again. He worked at the estate, didn't he?

The thought brought comfort she hadn't known she needed so terribly until now. She nestled beneath the covers, remembering each warm moment, each smile.

Until her father's disapproving face intruded upon the memories.

Go away! She dragged the pillow over her head.

Father could still present a problem. If he made trouble for Zack, everyone at Biltmore would dislike them, especially him. Normally, that sort of thing didn't bother her, but she would very much like for him to like her.

While she was here, of course.

Chapter Two

It was a problem Maddie thought she'd long overcome: waking up in a strange place and not remembering how she'd come to be there. The downy comfort of the bed and the warm fire crackling in the hearth were unfamiliar luxuries, almost too wonderful to be real.

Father's schemes never allowed them entry into wealthy circles. Until now.

Ah, yes. Biltmore castle.

Zack. The warmth of the blankets was nothing compared to being swooped up from an icy stream and held against his chest. He'd even carried her to this room.

The pleasant dreaminess shattered. Papa had ruined the man's good deed. And could still do worse.

Not if I have any say in the matter. She whipped back the blankets and readied herself in a hurry.

How had they gotten to this precarious point? Alfred Winterborn had learned of Vanderbilt's plan to decorate his castle with a medieval theme and hatched a scheme with another man to relieve the rich celebrity of some of his fortune. Somehow he'd convinced Vanderbilt of their connection to an English castle that had fallen on hard times and was being forced to sell some of its tapestries and suits of armor and such.

Overwhelming desire for such treasures often blinded people until it was too late. Could Vanderbilt be such a fool?

Maddie never claimed to be clairvoyant, but there was an undeniable sense of danger this time. As if they were on the edge of a precipice and about to tumble into the great unknown.

She, for one, intended to meet the unknown head on and prevent whatever disaster awaited her father. Smoothing her dress, she inhaled a bracing breath and then peeked down the hall. But where to find him?

Distant noises echoed, the clatter of dishes, the hushed tones of conversation. Servants, probably. Mr. Vanderbilt would make his presence known. As would her father.

She wouldn't find him by simply standing there in the hallway. She followed the sounds of activity, slowly at first. At footsteps behind her, she fell into the old practice of pretense. If she acted like she belonged at Biltmore, no one would question it.

Like a thousand times before, she assumed the persona of someone else. Someone with dignity and grace. By the time she walked into the dining hall, she was that girl.

"Good morning, Father." Relief washed over her. She was fairly certain the man who sat opposite him at the table was not Vanderbilt.

"Finally, you're awake. I was going to have someone check on you to be certain you hadn't fallen into a coma after hitting your head yesterday."

This was going to be more difficult than she thought. "Nonsense. As I told you, I'm perfectly fine. The whole thing was entirely my fault." She aimed an aren't-I-the-silly-one smile at the man. "My apologies. I'm Maddie Winterborn."

The man rose and bowed. "Pleasure to meet you, miss. Richard Morris Hunt, at your service."

"The architect of this impressive castle. How lovely to meet you." She curtsied, glad she'd paid attention to her father's ramblings.

She took her seat, feigning interest in their conversation as Hunt explained the dire need for the tapestries and castle accoutrements promised by her father. "Christmas will be upon us before you know it. The castle must be perfect by then."

Papa had a serious air. "Of course, of course. Everything will be in place for the Christmas Eve celebration." He turned to Maddie. "The grand opening of the castle."

She infused her "mmm" with enthusiasm, but was anything but. By that time, she and Papa would have to flee Asheville or risk imprisonment. She turned her focus to the plate of eggs, sausage, and toast as Hunt peppered her father with questions about delivery dates, and her father danced around the specifics with practiced ease.

The clock chimed ten. Hunt, explaining he had a business meeting, excused himself.

Papa dabbed a napkin to his mouth. "I, too, have a meeting."

"I thought your appointment with Vanderbilt was this afternoon."

"It is. I intend to seek out the person in charge of the driver."

She steeled her grip on the utensils. "For what purpose?"

"You know why."

She pinned him with a look of warning. "No, Father. That is completely unnecessary." Somehow, she'd kept her tone even and flat, in case any servants were nearby.

He hissed, "And I told you—"

"I will deny any accusation you make." There was plenty of blame to go around.

He drew back and looked at her as if she had morphed into someone unrecognizable.

Perhaps she was different. She might point out that, had he not abandoned her, the accident would not have happened. Instead, she used his standard instruction. "We should stick to the business at hand."

He tapped the table. "You'd do well to remember that."

"Whatever do you mean?" Barely an attempt at pleasantness.

A wince became an attempt at a grin. "Dalliances are troublesome. I'd hoped you'd learned that lesson."

She expelled an uneven breath and placed her hands against the table to steady herself. "The same could be said for greed." Her whisper must have penetrated his smugness. He flinched. Yes, her words might have stung, but she knew better than to think she'd wounded him.

He narrowed his eyes to glittering beads. "Let's walk, shall we?"

Not a request, she knew. "Perfect." Just what they both needed to clear the air.

After they fetched their overcoats, they strolled outside and along the walkway, newly constructed and not quite finished. When no one else was in sight, she still kept her voice low. "We are here to finish our work and leave without incident. That goal is in jeopardy." At least she had the sense to recognize it even if he didn't.

"How so?"

"We are in over our heads, Father."

He soured. "For very different reasons, it would seem."

"For the exact same purpose. To complete our mission unscathed. If we lose focus, we lose everything." The estate itself should have been proof enough. "Never have we dealt with such wealth." Where others surely saw an expansive landscape and impressive manor, Maddie saw danger. "Any man with such an investment would know how to protect his fortune. And prosecute any thief who attempted to steal it away."

"No need to worry, my sweet." His tone held anything but sweetness. "You concentrate on our work, and everything will be fine."

How could he be so blind? Her argument was cut short by a call from somewhere down the path.

Papa soured. "There he is. Your savior."

Father's sarcasm did not surprise her, but the flutter in her heart did. That she could so easily abandon their argument and welcome his intrusion with a bright smile surprised her more.

"Mr. Winterborn." Zack addressed her father with utmost respect. "Good morning." He tipped his hat to her. There was the hint of a smile, a bit of mischief in his expression.

The brightness of his greeting stole the morning chill.

"I trust you slept well?" he asked her.

"Very well." She stifled a grin.

"What is it?"

"You have a bit of…" She cupped his face, wiped her glove on his cheek. "There. Just some dirt." Again.

She found her hand in his.

"You shouldn't dirty your glove." Apparently

realizing his gaffe, he released her. "My normal condition, sadly. A hazard of the job."

She tilted her head up at him. "Driving a wagon?"

"I only do that occasionally, when the need arises. I'm actually the landscape engineer." He grew sheepish. "Well, one of them."

"Engine? In a landscape?" Her gaze wandered across the gardens and beyond.

"Not like that. It's easier if I show you. If you have time for a tour."

Her father huffed. "Perhaps some other—"

"I'd love one." Maddie stepped closer. "If you need to prepare for your meeting, Father…"

The world around them disappeared when she beamed up at Zack. She almost didn't hear her father say through gritted teeth, "It can wait. By all means, let's go," then climbed into the wagon without further argument. In the back seat, no less.

Which meant Maddie could ride alongside Zack. He wasted no time in assisting her to climb aboard. This time, she clutched his hand tightly.

"Chop-chop. I don't have all day." Her father was more than impatient. He was suspicious.

Zack ensured she was fully seated before propelling himself into the driver's side.

The image of grace, Maddie did her best to appear comfortable and pleasant while Zack climbed into his place beside her. What a terrible impression she must have made on the poor man when first they met.

And now her father was intent on putting them both in a poor light. She would have to counter his efforts.

Luckily, Zack appeared not to notice any subterfuge as he conducted the tour of the estate. With utmost good nature, he pointed out various areas and went on about the plan of the landscape designer, Frederick Olmsted.

For nearly everything Zack told them, Father had a question. Maddie knew what he was doing—trying to figure out the man's scam. Everyone worked a scam, whether big or small. Her father had taught her that early. The knowledge saved her from making a few huge mistakes in her life. No one deserved trust, he said, and she still found it difficult to give it away.

But was that true even of someone with genuine charm, like Zack? She made a point of studying him as he spoke with her father. No matter how Papa phrased his questions, Zack answered with cheerful enthusiasm. The more genuine Zack was, the more intent her father grew. She could almost hear the inner workings of his brain, trying to figure out the man's game. What her father didn't seem to fathom was the possibility there was no game. Just refreshing honesty.

This outing was a much-needed breath of fresh air, both literally and figuratively. Zack was a far cry from their normal business companions.

She was thoroughly enjoying herself until her father snapped to attention at Zack's mention that he couldn't find enough of the exotic and rare Franklinia and Persian ironwood trees that Olmsted envisioned for the space. "He also wants laurel, rhododendron, native azaleas and white pines. It doesn't look like much now, but on four acres over there, we'll have a Walled Garden, where thousands of flowers will grow in spring, summer and autumn. Then there'll be the All-American Rose Garden."

Father tapped the back of the bench in his usual *Eureka!* fashion. "I know just the man to help. He has what you need and more."

Not a stroke of genius, she knew. She was half-tempted to ask, *What man? When had they met?*

Zack glanced back. "He won't have a problem with the quantity?"

"Not at all. He runs a large plantation just south."

Confusion turned Zack's smile wan. "Where? I thought I knew all the nurserymen within a hundred miles."

"Farther south. Unlikely you'd have heard of him." Father carried off his smug expression with utter confidence.

Maddie caught Zack's hesitation, the second of doubt that crossed his face. But then Zack went on about the particular items he needed. Her father assured the man all would be provided. For a price, of course.

Her heart sank. None of what she'd said earlier had swayed her father. Papa was at the helm of their ship, and he was after the great White Whale, George Vanderbilt.

If she couldn't divert her father, their ship would soon be at the bottom of the sea.

The drive ended all too soon. Maddie stood outside the oversized house, so large it might swallow her up. And Papa, too.

She might have been standing outside a glass bubble as she watched him chatting up Zack, shaking his hand, so sure of himself. Oblivious to the danger they were in. To the danger he was putting them in. Had she believed he might listen, she'd plead with him to leave now, while they had the option to do so.

That would only annoy him, so she remained silent.

Not until she realized Zack was staring did she realize their conversation had ended.

"What do you have planned for the day?" he asked.

A very good question. "Nothing, really." She was expected to wait while her father conducted business.

"If you're looking for a book to read, Mr. Vanderbilt has plenty in his library. I'm sure he wouldn't mind if you borrowed one."

"How kind. Thank you." The house didn't appear quite so daunting, with a library inside somewhere.

"I'd offer to bring you, but the housekeepers frown when I track dirt inside." He gestured to the butler at the front entrance. "Mr. Booth? Would you mind showing Miss Winterborn to the library?"

The stately gent surveyed her. "Not at all. This way, miss."

Exhilaration washed over her. Free from the bonds of expectation, she could do as she wished.

"Maddie," Her father spoke as if to a forgetful pup.

She turned to him long enough to say, "Have a good meeting, Father."

"Don't get too caught up in your…reading."

Indignation swelled up, but she fought it back. She could say the same about his "business."

"Quite." The crisp word hung in the air, and she left it behind. An adventure awaited, if only literary.

She followed the butler, who threw open the wooden doors to a library such as she'd never seen. "Oh! How marvelous!"

A marvel indeed. Books packed the shelves, which ran from floor to ceiling. A very high ceiling. At one end, a spiral staircase allowed for browsing the titles on the second and third levels. Cherubs floated across the ceiling in a beautiful mural. A red velvet sofa and several matching chairs scattered the room.

"Where do I begin?"

"Anywhere you like." A bow, and he backed out of the room.

Giddy as a school girl, she wandered to the nearest case. More books than anyone could read in a lifetime! She could live in this room and devour them, one by one. Unable to choose only one, she closed her eyes and let her fingertips wander, then slid out a volume. After taking a place on the red velvet settee, Moby Dick engrossed her, chapter by chapter, so that when the large animal silently padded in and sat in front of her, she startled.

"Oh my. You gave me such a fright!"

The oversized canine's tail thumped the carpet. A friendly monster, at least.

"Who are you? Such a dashing gent." She scratched behind his ear, then turned the tag on his collar and read, " 'Cedric.' A regal name indeed."

The Saint Bernard widened his doggy smile.

"You seem in need of some fresh air. Would you like to go outside?"

Tail wagging, Cedric stood. A smart fellow, too.

"Right, then." She noted the page number and rested the book on the side table. "Off we go." There would be time enough to read later, when she'd need a distraction from her father's "business" dealings.

****

Autumn was the time to prepare the land for spring growing season, and that time was running short. Zack needed to focus on the job at hand until the estate was primed for the next growing season. Mr. Vanderbilt expected everything to be ready for his grand opening at Christmas.

No matter how he tried to concentrate, Zack couldn't get Maddie off his mind. Her father, too, but for a different reason. She may have wanted to act standoffish, but he could tell that cold exterior was a pretense, probably for her father's sake. The man was insufferable. A farm that carried everything Biltmore could need? Balderdash. Winterborn was about the shiftiest liar he'd ever met.

How had Mr. Vanderbilt not seen through the false promises?

What to do, what to do? If Zack went to Vanderbilt and even hinted at his suspicions, Maddie could also get in trouble. But if he didn't, and Winterborn stole the thousands Vanderbilt offered without producing the goods, he'd never forgive himself. A real pickle, it was.

Any scenario he devised to interrupt her didn't play out in his head the right way. He'd nearly given up when she came outside with Vanderbilt's dog, Cedric, newly arrived at the estate. She bent to the ground, threw something, and the hound bounded after it. More slowly, Cedric returned to her, tail a-wag and mouth wide in something like a canine smile. He hid a laugh behind his hand when she wrestled with the dog a bit, then pointed. Cedric sat. Another jab of her finger, and the stick dropped from Cedric's mouth.

He leaned on his shovel with a grin. "I didn't take you for an animal lover."

"Or vice versa. This sweet beast found me first."

"His name's Cedric."

She scratched the dog's cheeks. "Is he yours?"

"Noooo. He's the new pet of Mr. Vanderbilt. They both moved in last week."

She stepped back, glanced around. "Oh, I had no

idea. I apologize."

"For what? Keeping his dog entertained while he's busy settling in?"

"I must admit, I rather enjoyed it myself. But..." She lowered her voice. "You don't think he'll mind, do you?"

"How could he?" The master had let the canine out of his sight, and Maddie had taken good care of the pup. Truth was, though, Zack couldn't speak for Vanderbilt. "But what about your reading? Didn't you find a good book?"

"A very engrossing book."

"Which one?" He leaned on the shovel. Not some fluff fiction, he hoped.

"*Moby Dick*. The first line caught me up, and it didn't let go. Have you read it?"

"Yes. It's quite the tale. A cautionary one." Was that the attraction to it?

She let out a deep breath and took in their surroundings. "Does autumn always have such a lovely scent in Asheville?"

Interesting that she chose to avoid his comment. "In every season, actually."

"It's such a beautiful day."

In the sunlight, her auburn hair had a glorious sheen. A breeze sent a lock across her forehead, and she tucked it back, her smile angelic.

A sharp whistle cut the air. Cedric perked his ears, and ran to the side of the house, where Vanderbilt stood. The man gave no acknowledgement of Maddie or Zack, and then dog and owner disappeared from view.

An awkward moment of silence passed, then she said, "I should let you get back to work. I've no excuse for not reading now."

"Unless," he blurted, "you want to accompany me? I need to inspect part of the property. I could use the company."

She ducked her chin, and his heart fell. He knew the sign all too well. She was about to tell him no.

When she tilted her head up at him, her face was alight. "How can I refuse on such a fine day?"

A flutter in his chest reminded him to move before she changed her mind. "Give me five minutes to hitch up a horse."

Limbs jangling, he somehow managed to harness the horse and jumped into the wagon. He told himself to calm down, stop acting like a schoolboy, but still felt fit to bust out of his skin. She might have been a princess outside the castle, awaiting her carriage. But he had nothing regal to offer her, only a simple work wagon. Why she agreed to an outing with him, he couldn't understand.

When he halted the horse and helped her climb into the wagon, it brought to mind the last time he'd given a tour to her, and her father. Loyalty demanded he use this opportunity to learn more about the two of them, and their true motives. The thought left a bad taste in his mouth. Still, he owed as much to Vanderbilt.

He pointed out the reflecting pool that would one day occupy the rough patch of dirt in the front of the estate, bordered by the Italian Garden. They rode along in pleasant silence until they came upon another area of turned-over earth. He tied up the reins, drew out the landscape drawings and made some notes. So much left to be done, but it would take time to plant all the trees, bushes and flowers, and for them to fill in the landscape. Then it would look magnificent.

Her sigh drew his attention. "Sorry. This part's boring."

"Not at all. The scenery's beautiful. I was just wondering."

Now she had him wondering. "What?"

"What made you want such an occupation?"

There was no judgment in her question, but it wasn't the one he expected. "I feel a real connection to the land. There's nothing more satisfying than seeing a plan come to fruition." He detested braggarts, and yet here he was, trying to impress her again.

"I can certainly see how it would."

Her response struck him as thoughtful, as if she were used to a very different sort of plan. Before he could think of a question to address that, she spoke.

"It must be wonderful to design a landscape, fill it with trees and flowers, and watch them grow and thrive."

A deep sense of satisfaction filled him. "And provide a nurturing habitat for wildlife, too."

" 'I went to the woods because I wished to live deliberately.' "

His glance questioned her.

She explained, "Henry David—"

"Thoreau. Yes, I've read *Walden*." So she read a wide range of topics. Impressive.

"Are you of the same mind as Thoreau, then? That nature supersedes wealth?"

"Absolutely. What good is gold if we can't enjoy it in a wonderful place such as this?"

He slanted a smile her way.

Her cheeks flushed, and she ducked her head. "I agree."

Grin in place, he turned his attention back to the road

ahead. "You're different when you're away from your father."

"Am I? How so?"

"Less guarded. Easier to talk to." Except he sensed she put her guard up again.

"I suppose. Papa is overly protective."

Or her father's presence kept her in check so she didn't let any secrets slip. Rather than follow that thought, he simply made a noise of acknowledgement.

"Do you have something further to say?" She'd turned hard, her jaw set.

He'd definitely put her on edge. Innocent as a babe, he shrugged. "I only meant that you're more relaxed. Happier, in fact."

"Is that so." Nostrils flared, she stared ahead at the road.

She'd guarded herself against carelessness. He had to correct that, or she'd never let down that wall.

"You were, until I opened my mouth." He blew a breath. "I apologize. I overstepped."

"Quite right." Her glance still sharp, she visibly relaxed. "I will concede that you may be correct. Slightly. Being outside does put me in a good mood." She tilted her face to the sky. "I could drink up this sunshine."

The warmth chased away the chill from her attitude as well. "Is it true that England is mostly rainy?"

"I suppose. I haven't been there in a long time."

"Do you miss it?"

"My family, or what's left of them." She had a faraway look in her eyes. "My mother's gone, so we haven't been back in years."

Now he'd done it. Dredged up a painful past. "I'm

sorry. It must be very hard to be away from loved ones."

Her blinks fluttered, and the smile she sent had a sorrowful edge.

A rough patch dried his throat, and he had trouble swallowing. "I'd better get you back before your father misses you."

A small huff escaped, and he snuck a glance at her. Did she doubt that her father would miss her? If she did, she seemed resigned to it. He couldn't tell either way from her expression.

He drew back the reins near the front entrance to Biltmore and helped her step down. He imagined his hands at her waist, spinning her round, making her laugh. Instead, he'd caused her to remember sorrowful memories.

"Thank you. It's been lovely." Her big, brown eyes crinkled when she looked up at him.

Did she forgive him? The weight of their earlier conversation eased, somehow. Standing with her, he forgot the manners his Pap had instilled in him. He wanted to stay there and get lost in those eyes.

Someone called his name, and the moment broke. He turned to ask the intruder to wait, but she slipped inside.

Will took hold of the halter and led the horse toward the barn. "Did you get what you needed?"

Anger welled up, but Will's innocence brought Zack to his senses. Will Culpepper had every right to ask about the job he'd set out to finish. He was, after all, the assistant groundskeeper.

"Not yet." Not his work for Vanderbilt, or the questions that burned in his mind about Mr. Winterborn. "But I will." No matter how unpleasant the task, he must see it through. Whatever the outcome, he'd do his best to protect Maddie.

She was the only one he could trust to answer truthfully.

He had to find a way to get her alone again. Next time, he'd keep a tighter rein on his senses.

****

The grandfather clock chimed three times. *Three?* How had time escaped her? Every time Maddie was with Zack, it seemed to happen. They'd begin talking, or simply enjoy an amiable quiet between them, and hours slipped past.

A vague intent to find the book she'd abandoned brought her back to the library. Behind the closed doors, two men spoke: her father's smooth, easy voice under rode the other man's curt one. Mr. Vanderbilt, she presumed.

Father once told her his voice was his magic. He could convince anyone of anything, for as long as necessary.

Usually. Today seemed to be the exception. Vanderbilt fired back before her father finished his sentences.

The niggling thought that this "job" would end in disaster had haunted her since the train ride. Vanderbilt's wealth afforded him tremendous power and influence, which undoubtedly stretched beyond the borders of North Carolina. Perhaps even beyond the United States. If the deal went sour, she and her father might be on the run a very long time. If they could outrun trouble of this magnitude.

She retreated to her room and regretted leaving the copy of *Moby Dick* on the library table. Mr. Vanderbilt likely wouldn't have minded if she borrowed the book to read, but she didn't feel right without first asking.

Instead, she sat in the chair beside the fireplace and made do with Emily Dickinson. The poems always made her feel closer to her mother.

Strangely enough, so did talking with Zack. When she'd told him about her mother's death, a flood of memories washed over her and left her with a lasting warmth, even though many of them had to do with Christmas. Mama pulling her on the little wooden sled, both of them laughing. Mama teaching her how to string paper garland over the doorways and around the tree. Mama holding her high so she could place the star atop the highest bough.

A tear streaked her cheek, but she was smiling when she wiped it away. Her memories portrayed England in a brighter light, mostly because, in her memories, Mama smiled back at her.

Zack had helped her remember things she'd tried not to think about for many years. He'd spoken truths she worked hard to deny, but he'd spoken her truth. A truth that pierced her heart, but in a strangely welcome way. He helped her remember the wonderful parts of her childhood. Each time, her heart opened a little more.

She had wanted to thank him, but a lump in her throat stopped her from speaking. Every time she was with him, it seemed some emotion she'd kept buried managed to bubble to the surface. And it wasn't entirely a bad thing.

The knot inside her loosened when she was near him. She could almost be herself.

If only she knew who that self truly was. She'd been pretending for too long.

She went to the window and hoped for a glimpse of him. Would he call on her again? Or would Father prevent any further encounters because he needed her to divert attention from his schemes?

How nice that someone looked out for her, especially someone as good-hearted as Zack.

Maybe this holiday would be a good one after all. If she could convince Papa to stay in Asheville a bit longer than planned. She would be very sorry indeed to leave so soon.

The hallway echoed with loud conversation. Mr. Vanderbilt, insistent and terse. Her father, solicitous as ever. Each promise to fulfill Vanderbilt's wishes louder, and then he burst inside, leaned against the door and mopped his brow with his handkerchief.

"Are you all right?"

He strode toward the credenza, opened a decanter and sniffed. Then the next, and finally the last one. "Ugh. Is there no liquor?"

"Not in my room, no." A stern approach might work. "What is going on?"

He took the chair opposite, barely perched on the seat. "Vanderbilt insists we have his merchandise here in a few weeks."

We? She let that pass.

"He kept going on and on about how everything must be perfect for his grand opening at Christmas."

Yes, Christmas. The one Father promised would be so special. It wasn't looking so promising.

"How will you manage?" She wanted to emphasize *you* but decided against it.

"Very carefully." His foot bounced. "Timing will be tricky indeed."

A sudden weariness came over her. Too many years of deals and schemes and, in the end, having to run away to the next city to do it all over again.

"Can this time be the last?" She hadn't meant to say it out loud, but there it was.

He finally looked at her. "You can't be serious. And then what?"

Then we have a normal life, she wanted to tell him. Would he even remember how?

He pushed to his feet. "I must get to town." And then he was in the hall, his footsteps receding.

And what must I do, Father? Sit mute as a porcelain doll and wait?

She refused to lock herself away in this room, however elegant it might be. A walk would help clear her head.

A good thirty minutes later, the sun was descending toward the horizon and she had wandered off the walkway. Biltmore looked more like an oversized doll house. "Oh, dear." She'd let her temper carry her too far.

A chipmunk scampered across her path. Leaves rustled, perhaps from a larger animal? A chill crept up the back of her neck. Nightfall would bring true cold.

She tugged her collar up and aimed for the castle. Her stomach growled, a reminder she'd missed lunch, and dinner was in danger of the same fate.

Noises from the trees sent her rushing ahead. Her boot caught on a tree root, and she tumbled to her knees. Something sharp dug into her calf, and she sat on the cold ground to inspect the wound. Nothing too serious, but blood trickled down her leg. Wild animals would home in on such a raw scent. She needed to hurry.

The longer she walked, the more her leg throbbed.

She hobbled to put less pressure on it. Shadows deepened around her. Lights shone from the Biltmore windows. It did rather resemble a castle. One she wished to be inside.

In the darkness, an animal snorted. She held her breath to listen. *Hooves.* Someone on horseback.

"Hello?" she called. *Please hear me.* "Hello!"

"Miss Winterborn?" A man, unfamiliar to her.

"Maddie!" called a more familiar voice.

She released a breath. *Zack.* "Here! I'm over here!"

Goliath pranced to her in a majestic sidestep.

"Thank goodness." Zack leapt off. "Are you hurt?"

On the other horse rode Paddy Curthbert, the stable master, who pulled to a stop beside Goliath.

"I'm fine." She took a step, and pain shot through her leg. "Actually, my leg is less than fine."

"Let me help." Hand at her waist, he supported her, then lifted her into the saddle, then swung up behind her.

After he took up the reins, his arms acted as two shields. "Hold tight." He clicked the horse to a trot.

She gripped the saddle horn and relaxed against him. "Right. Bad enough you had to rescue me twice. We don't want to have a third."

His laugh rumbled in his chest, and she rather liked it.

"I don't mind," he said close to her ear. "Not one bit."

From the other horse, Paddy said, "Shouldn't make a habit of late walks, miss. Bear have been sighted these past weeks."

"Bear?" She twisted to see Zack, to see if Paddy might be joking, but darkness had engulfed them, and she could hardly make out his features.

"They're readying to hibernate." He sounded

serious. "They're filling their bellies with whatever they can."

"Tell them English girls are too sour."

"I find them sweet." His smile came through in his voice.

"I guess I wouldn't know," came the pitiful reply from the other horse.

Maddie couldn't hold back a laugh. "Count your blessings," she told Paddy.

Within a few minutes, they reached the main house. Zack jumped down, and held out his arms.

Maddie slid into them. "Thank you. Again." She started to the entrance, and winced.

"Let me help."

She might have protested, if she weren't enjoying his arm around her as they walked.

He guided her to the far kitchen, nearest the staff hallway. "How long were you out walking?"

"I'm not sure, really. I needed to think."

He made that sound, the one that bewildered and angered her. The one that indicated either agreement, or skepticism. Did he not believe her?

"Annie always makes too much food. I'm sure we can find some for you."

"Only if you'll join me." In her mind, an image of her alone in the kitchen was too pathetic.

"Happy to."

He did appear to be, she thought. Warmth spread through her, and she thought perhaps that might be happiness, too. Her father would say that was a luxury neither of them could afford.

Tonight, she wanted to indulge in it, if only for a short while.

No sooner had she sat on the kitchen stool than Annie appeared.

"I thought I heard someone. Do you need something?"

"Food," said Zack. "But first, do you have something to clean a wound?"

The cook bustled to a cabinet. "I've some antiseptic, and gauze, if you need it." She hurried over and set down the supplies.

His face flushed red. "Would you mind?" He turned his back.

Maddie hiked her skirt. "It's just a scratch, I'm sure."

Annie set to work. "A bit deeper than a scratch, but this will work nicely."

The liquid stung, but Maddie held back any complaint. "You're so kind. Thank you."

After gathering her supplies again, Annie returned them to their shelf. "Help yourself to leftovers. There's roast beef, with potato and carrots and onions. Delicious, if I say so myself."

"Thanks, Annie." Zack peeked at Maddie. "All better?"

"Yes, perfect."

"Except you're hungry. So am I."

She cleared her head of worry and let herself enjoy the moment. She watched him prepare two plates, and smiled her thanks when he slid one plate in front of her. "Lovely. *Merci beaucoup.*"

He took the stool beside her. "French, eh?"

"I only speak a little." Father hadn't allowed them enough time in France to fully learn the language. He was always in too much of a rush to get to the next job, the next place.

"Have you been? I've heard it's a beautiful country."

"I was young." Time to change the subject. "What about you?"

"Maybe someday I'll visit." His pleasant expression wavered, and he pushed the fork around his plate. "Maddie."

Oh, dear. This was not going the way she'd hoped. "Yes?"

He studied her a moment. "I hate to ask, but I have to."

"What is it?" She braced for the worst.

"Can your father honestly obtain all the items Vanderbilt asked for?" He turned sheepish. "And the ones Olmed needs, too? Those Franklinia and Persian ironwood trees are really rare. I haven't heard of anyone nearby who grow them."

She could tell by the way he phrased the question so carefully, he didn't want to offend her. Yet he needed answers.

The more she stared into his face, the face of an honest, hard-working man, she couldn't muster the casual cover-ups she so often had used to defend her father. She just couldn't lie to Zack.

But she could explain.

Appetite gone, she set down her fork, and smoothed the napkin across her lap. "When my mother died, my father nearly did, too. Of grief. Eventually, he came back to me, but he was never the same. He was a broken man. He pulled himself together because he was desperate to take care of me the way Mama wanted." She didn't know why she was telling him these things. Maybe it was her way of begging forgiveness for him. For them both.

He nodded, as though he knew exactly what she meant. Hope flickered in her breast, tempered by his troubled expression. He stared at his hands as if an answer could be deciphered in the weathered lines of his palm. For a long time, they said nothing.

Maddie knew not to push him. They had put Zack in a terrible spot. He was responsible for maintenance of the land. Papa had gone too far in promising to deliver the goods Zack needed. When her father failed to deliver, Zack would be blamed. He would lose his job that he loved so well. Not only that, but his reputation. Many others had seen him with her, laughing together. Colluding, some might say. It wouldn't take long for rumors to spread that Zack had been part of the scam. People were so cruel that way.

He pushed to his feet as if he carried a heavy burden. "I'd better say good night." He set the plate on the floor for Cedric to finish what he couldn't.

"I'll finish cleaning up." She could barely wish him a good night. He'd likely toss and turn in his bed, wrestling with how to do the right thing without hurting her. "Thank you again, Zack. You'll never know how much I appreciate your help."

He stared a moment, as if trying to decipher whether her words had some underlying message. She held his gaze, trying to assure him she wouldn't ask him for anything. He'd done enough.

A nod, and he seemed to struggle with whether to leave or stay. But they both knew what he had to do. He left.

Now there was only one thing for her to do. Roust her father from his too-comfortable bed and steal away

in the dead of night.
    Tonight.
    Better to ruin Papa's plans than his life.

Chapter Three

Good thing Goliath knew the way back to Biltmore. Zack could think of nothing besides the morning's visit to Doc Jackson. Just a check-up, supposedly, until the doctor was unable to make a real diagnosis about Pa. A pain in his chest could be from stress, Doc had said, but Zack suspected something worse. Any guilt about showing up late to work vanished.

When he returned, Will Culpepper looked surprised. "You're here."

The few hours of sleep grated Zack's nerves, too. "Where else would I be?" From Will's face, Zack guessed far from here. "What's wrong?"

"The Winterborns are gone."

"Gone?" He should have suspected something like that. The father, yes, but Maddie?

"Up and left in the middle of the night. Mr. Vanderbilt sent Elijah to the train station to catch up to them."

"Maybe they just went to town for something." The moment he said it, Zack knew he was wrong.

Will shook his head. "When Mrs. Elliott knocked on the girl's door this morning, they found an envelope on the dresser, and a note."

"A note?"

"Addressed to you." He kicked at the dirt. "Along with a pile of cash."

"What?" Zack could hardly think straight. "What did she say?"

Will shrugged. "Mostly, that she was sorry."

Of course, she wouldn't have said where they were headed. She would protect her father, but that meant she'd disappear along with him.

Zack would never see her again. That hit him hard, almost knocking the wind from him.

He ran a hand through his hair. "When is Elijah due back?" He might have learned something of their whereabouts.

"He left a few hours ago, so should be back soon."

Zack looked for any activity around the house, but nothing appeared amiss. "I better go find Mrs. Elliott, and see what's what."

The urge to find out sent him into a jog. He entered through the main kitchen. Annie spun around from her tête-à-tête with the butler.

Annie smoothed her apron. "Mr. Kingley."

"Morning, Annie. Giles." He tipped his hat to them both. "Is Mrs. Elliott busy?"

Giles gestured to the hall. "In her office, I believe."

"Much appreciated." He strode in that direction, and because the door was already open, knocked on the frame. "Morning, Mrs. Elliott."

Her head snapped up from her papers. "Mr. Kingley. I hadn't expected to see you."

"Seems to be a common misconception around here. I took my father to see Doc Jackson in town this morning, so I missed all the excitement. I heard you may have a note addressed to me?"

"So you knew nothing about their plan?"

Zack found it hard to believe there was a plan. Or if

so, it was a hastily put-together one. "I wish I did." He might have been able to stop them. Or her, at least.

A few brisk blinks as she assessed him, and then Mrs. Elliott opened the desk drawer and drew out a folded paper. "I apologize for reading this. There was no seal."

That was no excuse, but he was sure Vanderbilt would not object to his head housekeeper reading his personal message, so he could hardly object, either. "She left an envelope, too?"

"As you'll see in her letter, the money is to repay Mr. Vanderbilt. Though it's hardly close to the real total, I should think."

His heart sank. At least she'd tried. He opened the folded sheet and skimmed the writing: *...sorry to leave so abruptly...gathered whatever I could from my father to repay Mr. Vanderbilt...never meant to hurt you...*

The last sent a pang through his heart. She had hurt him, surprisingly. A lot more than he'd care to admit.

He re-folded the letter. "Well." He cleared his throat. "Any word from Elijah?"

"Not yet."

"Will you keep me informed, please?"

"Of course."

"Much obliged."

Blasted bad timing. He'd go after her himself, but he couldn't leave Pa. Not now, when his father might need him most.

He had that much in common with Maddie, he supposed—they both dearly loved their fathers. He'd thought there was more than that, but maybe he'd read too much into her shy but flirtatious ways, and her smile wasn't truly meant to tell him he was the only one on earth. Just the most gullible.

"I'm such a fool!" He stomped into the main kitchen.

Annie startled again. Hand to her chest, she gasped. "Oh, Mr. Kingley! Is everything all right?"

"No, Annie. Not in the least." Not that he wanted to share his misfortune with anyone. He strode outside.

The sunshine mocked him, bright and cheery as it was, though a chill hung in the air.

Is she warm? Is she safe?

Stop! He chided himself. *I'm done with her.*

Or, she was done with him. It might take him a while to catch up.

****

The back of the wagon made for cramped quarters. Maddie didn't know how her father had found this traveling tradesman so fast. Actually, she did. He always had a bead on the shiftiest people in town.

The man was traveling north and was willing to let them ride in the back. For a price.

Then came a tense moment when her father struck a bargain to give the man half the money now, half when they reached their destination. Maddie's worries melted when he drew a money clip from inside his vest. That alone bought her some time.

And time was the commodity that was most critical.

The morning train would have arrived too late. Almost certainly, Vanderbilt would send someone to apprehend them.

So there they were, shoulders bumping in the dirty wagon bed.

Though Maddie hadn't asked, Papa announced, "Pittsburgh. That's where we're headed. Port to three rivers, so it's a busy trade city. We'll find something there." Disgust dripped from his tone.

"Pittsburgh," she dully repeated. By all accounts, freezing this time of year.

As usual, she put up a façade of pleasantness and hoped it didn't appear too worn. She was suddenly very tired of the mask she was forced to wear. And the constant moving from place to place.

No one questioned Father's British roots, with his unmistakable English accent, but after all their travels, Maddie worked to keep her accent. Born outside London, her first ten years were bliss, with Father a successful accountant and doting husband and Mama a loving wife and parent. Mama's death changed everything. Locked in grief, Father had allowed debtors to chip away at their possessions until, finally, they had no house. Ten years of travel had sharpened Father's skills. Now Maddie thought of her homeland as a fairytale place but felt little connection to England. She wasn't sure where she belonged anymore.

And what of Papa? He couldn't possibly enjoy the life he forced upon them both. What kept him at it? And why face off against such a man as George Washington Vanderbilt? To run afoul of such a powerful person, in a rural town, could lead to the worst trouble they'd seen. So far, luck had seen them through scrapes, if only by the skin of their teeth.

She'd wished for an old-fashioned Christmas for her birthday, but now she considered she should change that wish for luck enough to see them through.

These were the thoughts that ran through her head with her father silent and cold beside her.

"We'll have a fresh start." He shifted and pulled out

his billfold, and stared into the empty cavity. In disbelief, he reached inside. "What happened...where is my money?"

She swallowed hard as she sat straight. "In an envelope on the dresser in my room." Likely already discovered and handed to Zack, as she'd addressed it to him. She trusted him to hand the cash over to Mr. Vanderbilt.

His eyes flinched. Then his mouth. "You stole from me?"

"It wasn't yours." Maddie was too numb to think. The cash she'd left didn't cover Vanderbilt's losses. What would happen to Zack? Would Vanderbilt blame him for the lost money? Oh no, what if she'd unwittingly made him look like an accomplice in the scheme?

"Once we reach Pittsburgh, you'll pay me back, missy."

Suddenly, her life stretched out before her. One scam after another, always on the run from the authorities and toward the next innocent target.

She knew what she had to do. Break from him, this very moment. If she didn't, she might end up trapped in this dead-end life. Always running to keep ahead of the last hustle and running to catch the next one.

She banged against the back of the seat where the tradesman sat. "Stop! Stop the wagon."

"We can't stop. We must keep moving."

She gathered her bag and scooted to the back. "Wrong, Papa. I'm returning to Biltmore. I intend to pay back Mr. Vanderbilt." Somehow. "Someday, I hope you'll learn to love yourself again the way Mama loved you."

He drew back, eyes flaring, as if slapped.

Pain split her heart. Did he not know how much she needed him to do the right thing? And to love her, too?

"Farewell, Father. God speed." A quick kiss to his cheek, and she turned on her heel, bag in hand, and struck out on foot down the road they'd traveled.

Hours dragged by. Her feet were numb. Her hands were numb with cold, and her arm ached from the weight of her bag. For once, she was glad for owning so few possessions.

She tried not to think about what awaited her. The unknown had a terrible face, but she would grow familiar with it, line by line, and conquer it.

If the bears didn't get her first.

****

The whisper of a rustle sounded in the hallway outside Zack's room. In the silence that followed, he thought he must have imagined it. Yet something made him move to the door and open it.

Hand raised to knock, Maddie stared, agape.

He threw his arms around her, twirled her. "You're all right. I was so worried."

A strangled noise erupted from her, so he set her down. "Sorry." He palmed her face. "What happened?"

Tears welled in her eyes, but she gulped them back. "You already know. I'll make no more excuses, either. I'm here to set things right. No matter how long it takes. If Mr. Vanderbilt needs another servant, I'll work and he can collect my wages every week until everything's repaid that my father took."

"Maddie…" If she only knew how many years such an offer entailed.

"Don't try to stop me, Zack. My father's gone, and I'll likely never see him again. It took me too long to break from him, but I'm here to do the right thing."

"You had no part in his scheme." He hoped.

"I knew what he planned to do. I've always known his work hurt people, but I couldn't let him hurt you. And I can't let you take the blame for my father's dishonesty, either."

Is that what she thought? "You don't need to—"

"Please, Zack. My mind is made up."

In truth, she appeared rattled but determined. "I can tell. I respect that." He slipped the bag from her steely grip.

"Did they give you the envelope on my dresser?"

"The note." His heart had both leapt and fell when he saw his name written on the outside. He thought he'd lost her for good.

"I don't know how much Mr. Vanderbilt paid my father, or the other man. I took whatever was in my father's billfold. It's a start, at least. But I'll work to pay off the rest."

Even the other fellow's half? How could he allow her to assume a debt that wasn't hers? "Let me see what I can do. In the meantime, we'll see about getting you settled." He drew her inside to a chair and bade her sit. "Remember: *Dwell in possibility.*"

The look of astonishment said she'd understood the message from Emily Dickinson. She had so many possibilities ahead. He wished he could list them all for her, show her she had the world at her feet.

For now, it was enough that she was here. On his way to Mrs. Elliott's office, it took all his self-control not to let out a whoop. Joy filled him to the point of bursting. She'd come back.

And he'd do his best to keep her safe from harm.

****

For the most part, Maddie had glimpsed Constance Elliott only at a distance, speaking with servants in a clipped voice. Now she was a formidable adversary.

Thank goodness Zack had acted the gentleman and escorted her. Her nerves might not have withstood the woman's harsh attitude otherwise.

"Against my better judgment, I'm told I should provide you with work." Mrs. Elliott narrowed her eyes. "Tell me why I should."

This was no time for pride. Only truth. Maddie looked her straight in the eye. "I'm hoping to right my father's wrong against Mr. Vanderbilt. He's a broken man who's lost his way. And I need to find my own path." She gulped. "The right path."

"Do you think you can?"

An honest question deserved an honest answer. "I will do my best."

The woman seemed less than impressed. "And what is it that you can do, Miss Winterborn?"

Cold splashed over Maddie. She had no idea. She'd only ever been good at shielding her father from harm.

Zack spoke up. "She's a good…cook?" He looked to her.

Maddie winced, shook her lowered head.

"Housekeeper," he tried.

Mrs. Elliott turned dour. "I've plenty waiting for such positions already." The woman began to turn away.

Maddie's heart raced. She was losing her only opportunity.

"None like Miss Winterborn," said Zack. "She's a hard worker, smart, and willing to learn. She deserves a chance."

Over her shoulder, Mrs. Elliott arched a brow. "Do you?"

Did she? Why not? Didn't everyone? "Yes."

"Then one chance is what you get." She whisked down the hall, calling, "Come along, if you're coming. Lucky for you, I'm hiring more staff in advance of the grand opening." She came to an abrupt halt, cast her eyes to the ceiling as if reading instructions there. "The bathrooms. We'll start you there."

"Thank you." So, she'd clean a few bathrooms.

"There are forty-three." The woman appeared to gauge her response.

"Oh." Maddie's heart fell, but she refused to be put off. So, she'd clean a lot of bathrooms. "All right." She'd put up with far worse conditions than Biltmore.

Apparently, Maddie had passed some sort of test. Mrs. Elliott begrudgingly admitted, "Only some are currently in use. You'll begin on the first floor."

Quaking like a leaf, Maddie stood tall. She must not let Zack see her crumple to pieces in the face of a challenge. He was a good and decent man, and she had to show him she could be such a person.

His brief touch at her elbow made her turn. He was leaving. She wanted to beg him to stay beside her, lend her the strength she needed.

But she suspected he'd tell her to find the strength within herself, and he'd be right. It was time for her to learn to do just that. On her own.

The hallway echoed with Mrs. Elliott's clipped footsteps. "First, you must have the proper uniforms."

Yes, she'd noticed the two different types—maids wore lavender dresses with white collars and cuffs during the day, and in the evening, changed to more formal black uniforms with white trim.

As she followed, Maddie noticed with new appreciation the polished floors and woodwork, gleaming fixtures, the furniture positioned just so throughout the home. Every bit of it thanks to the hard work of the Biltmore servants.

Expectation of everyone was set high, and she would work harder to meet Mrs. Elliott's standards. If she didn't, she would find herself on the street, penniless, or worse, in jail.

A few dirty bathrooms were worth it.

Chapter Four

How different it was to work inside the great house rather than to be welcomed as a visitor. Mr. Vanderbilt, she was told, did not like to be in the same room as the servants, so she must avoid a face-to-face encounter with him or risk dismissal. Fortunately, he traveled often; unfortunately, she was not aware of his schedule. Once, he strode past the narrow hallway reserved for servants when she was near, and she had to duck behind a grandfather clock until he passed. A chance meeting under her particular circumstance would be too embarrassing to bear. Did he even know about her situation? Had he given his blessing, or did Mrs. Elliott have free rein over hiring decisions?

Maddie would not tempt fate by asking. She faced enough difficulties in maintaining her precarious place within Biltmore.

Worse, the complete turnabout of the staff came as a shock. It shouldn't have surprised her that the others glared instead of smiled, or answered in clipped sentences and in harsh tones rather than soft, but somehow it unnerved her. Their disapproval of her hung in the air of every room. Conversations fell silent when she entered, and upon her departure from any group, hushed whispers followed her.

The first indication of the dark greeting awaiting her was when Mrs. Elliott called for Miss Appleton.

The dark-haired girl hurried over and halted on a curtsy. "Yes, ma'am."

"Since the dismissal of Miss Thayer, there's an empty bed in your room, correct?"

A more tentative, "Yes, ma'am."

"Good. Show Miss Winterborn there, and help her get settled." To Maddie, Mrs. Elliott said, "Change into your uniform and return at once."

Maddie caught Miss Appleton's keen glance, one that held disappointment and a warning.

"Yes, ma'am," Maddie mimicked the other girl. She wanted to add more, promises that the head housekeeper wouldn't be sorry, that Maddie would do her best, but Mrs. Elliott had briskly departed.

Miss Appleton turned on her heel. "Hurry. I've a full workload today."

Maddie hoisted her bag and hurried after the girl already rounding the corner. When she caught up, the girl was halfway up the first flight of stairs, her pace fast as she climbed. Three flights up, Maddie struggled to keep pace. Her legs burned and her palm ached from the tight grip on the bag's handles. She pushed through the discomfort but silently gave thanks when the girl headed to a door at the end of the hallway.

Maddie took in the room. A generous size, with two iron beds, two dressers, and two wardrobes of chestnut wood. For each of them, a washstand with pitcher, washbowl, and all the necessities, plus a chair.

"Only female staff live on this floor." The girl pointed to a neatly made single bed on the left side of the room. "That one's yours, and you can use the furniture beside it. The uniforms hanging on it should fit, more or less. Get changed and go back downstairs." She paused, her sharp gaze swept over Maddie. "You *can* find your way back, correct?"

"Yes. Yes, thank you so much. Please, call me Maddie."

The girl's mouth soured. "I'm Miss Appleton. Do *not* touch anything of mine. I will know if you do."

Flustered, Maddie managed, "No, of course I won't. I wouldn't."

An arched brow answered. "Hurry up. If you cross her, Mrs. Elliott can be mean as a polecat, and that's on a good day." She closed the door, and Maddie heard her mumble, "And this is not a good day."

As her footsteps receded, so did Maddie's hopes. No one wanted her here. What was she even doing?

She went to the window and peered out at the expansive grounds. Too late to run. She'd never get away from Biltmore without someone stopping her. Then she'd end up in jail. Possibly for life.

This was a different sort of prison, but one that might provide her a means of escape. If she worked very hard.

At least Zack believed in her. He must, or he wouldn't have brought her to Mrs. Elliott.

She'd proved to him that he hadn't misplaced his faith. That she was worthy. Then they would all see they were wrong about her.

A quick change into the uniform shook her confidence. The waist hung loose, and the sleeves covered her wrists. Still, she pinned back her hair and checked her reflection. With a nod, she rushed down the steps.

At the bottom of the staircase, Charlotte Payne and Phoebe Dawson watched her with glittering eyes. In passing, Mr. Booth the butler did a double-take, and his eyes widened before he doubled his pace.

No heroine's welcome for her. She honestly didn't expect one, but a friendly face would have helped.

"Has anyone seen Mrs. Elliott?" she asked the two women.

They turned up their noses and turned away as if she hadn't spoken.

"Don't bother yourselves. I'll find her on my own." That's how she'd have to do everything from now on— on her own.

She'd never felt so alone in her life.

****

"Where the blazes are the cherubs?" Zack heard how ridiculous he sounded, and so did most everyone else, the way folks in the train station turned to look his way. He hated barking at the man in that way, but he was tired of getting barked at himself. Olmsted blamed Zack for the delay, and held Zack responsible for delivery of the garden statuary. But as his father always said, *Ours is not to wonder why, ours is but to do or die.* And Zack didn't want to die on a hill full of cherubs.

"The shipment incurred a slight delay." The bespectacled man at the counter peered beady-eyed from behind the bars.

Likely the man was glad for those iron bars, the way Zack was ranting like a lunatic. He counted two beats, then steadied himself. "When, exactly, will they arrive?"

The clerk shuffled the papers in front of him, with frequent glances at Zack. "Thursday next."

A deliberate, slow nod, and Zack clarified, "The 14th of November, then."

More shuffling, more glances, then, "Yes." A

defiant mouse in its cage.

Zack might be tempted to feed the mouse to the giant lion at Biltmore, if only the lion were real and not another sculpture.

"All right. Then we will be back Thursday next." And meantime, he'd try to calm Olmsted, who'd do his best to reassure Vanderbilt. The cherubs would go a long way toward cheering them all.

Or so he kidded himself. There was so much left to do, Zack's head spun if he thought on it too long. So much land to prepare, shrubs and saplings to plant, and flower bulbs for spring.

Outside the station office, Zack jammed his hands into his pockets. "This means we'll lose more days to traveling back and forth." Though these days, he spent half his week on these fetch-and-deliver trips. Other days, he spent all his hours far from the castle, outside the Conservatory, the Italian Garden, everywhere but near the main residence, where he might catch a glimpse of Maddie. Guilt weighed on him heavier with each passing day he couldn't speak with her.

Will shifted uneasily at his side. "At least the larger statues are already in place."

"Thank the Greek gods for that." Faun, Adonis, Venus, and Hamadryad had stepped out of Greek mythology and looked right at home on the Biltmore lawns. Or what would be lawns, once the seed grew.

"The wagons will be full of shrubs and flowers and seed bags." Will was making an attempt to find the positive in a bad situation, as usual.

Zack made a low sound in his throat, neither agreement or disagreement. "If those supplies haven't met untimely delays too." A knot balled in his stomach at the thought. "We'd better go see."

"Mr. Vanderbilt's guests can't really expect the outdoors to be finished, can they? The indoors isn't even done yet."

"If Mr. Vanderbilt wants to make a good impression on his friends, we'll do our best to make it happen." So long as Vanderbilt understood Zack wasn't a miracle worker. He didn't need his four years of training in the Biltmore Forest School to remind him it would take years for the plantings to fully mature and look the way Olmsted presented them in his sketches. "I just want to get what we came for so we can get back."

"Yes, sir."

Zack couldn't tell if Will was being a smart ass or not. He looked more disappointed, the way he watched the wagons that passed.

The scent of cooked meat from a nearby eatery made Zack's mouth water. "You hungry? That beef smells mighty tempting."

"I could eat," Will said.

"Stay with the wagons. I'll be back in a few minutes." Zack dodged the barrage of traffic weaving both ways down the street. His eye caught a small table inside a small shop with books piled high, so he ducked inside. A copy of *Little Women* featured prominently.

Zack turned the book over in his hands, the gold lettering of the title worn and faded as the rest of the red cover. Had Maddie mentioned wanting to read this? She probably never got to start it. "How much?"

"Fifty cents."

The image on a green book cover, a sailboat rocking on the seas, drew him to that tome. "*The Adventures of Captain Horn?*"

"Did you like *Treasure Island? Robinson Crusoe?* You'll like this one." The seller behind the counter gave a knowing nod.

He might strike a deal with the man. "How much for both?"

The man didn't hesitate. "Both for one dollar."

Zack dug the coins from his pocket and exchanged them for the books. "Sold."

"Enjoy," the man called after him.

He slipped them inside his coat. He'd enjoy the look on Maddie's face when he gave them to her. Probably on Christmas. He had to look after Pa until he was steadier on his feet. Guilt wracked him for not visiting Maddie at the house, but Mrs. Elliott would surely count any such visit against her. She'd be better off if he left her alone, for now.

****

For nearly ten years, Maddie had known only a life on the road, traveling from town to town, sometimes crossing continents, always looking over her shoulder for a telltale sign someone followed, gauging the expressions of those around them, on alert for cues that danger lurked nearby. Rarely had she slept in the same room, in the same bed, for more than a week.

She used to wonder if a regular routine would grow tedious, if the same surroundings every day would bore her. After these past weeks at Biltmore, she could attest that the opposite was true. Tonight, like every night, she found comfort in returning her head to the same pillow. In the bed opposite, Sophie Appleton reclined on her side, with her back to Maddie.

Snuggled beneath the covers, Maddie kept her attention on her book. She knew the lines by heart but still savored each one, all the while keenly aware of another presence. The library.

Though several floors beneath, it pulsed like a live being, breathing with endless possibilities, each title an entryway to another world in which she could explore, make friends, and feel accepted.

If only she could borrow some books from those shelves. Likely it was better she was not allowed, or else she might stay up all night, too engrossed in a new story to sleep. Then she wouldn't have the energy to fulfill her work duties, and then...

"It's past time for the light to go out." The muffled scold came from Sophie's bed.

Maddie repressed an argument. "Sorry." With a sigh, she set the book on the night table and put out the light. "Sleep well."

She knew better than to expect a reply. She'd wished her roommate the same sentiment every evening but received not so much as a scowl in reply.

How long would it take to earn the trust of the others? Would they ever befriend her? Or even tolerate her?

A stray tear fell to her pillow, and she swiped her eyes. Self-pity would get her nowhere.

Light barely streaked the morning sky when the knock came. "Time to rise." Footsteps, then the same knock and the same greeting was repeated at each door.

When the light in their room winked on, Maddie winced. Sophie was already dressing. Her glance advised Maddie to do the same.

Maddie had always been a light sleeper and early riser. Once though, just once, she'd have liked to sleep in for a bit. If she did so any day at Biltmore, she'd have no breakfast, and regular meals had become another highlight of her day. She no longer had to scavenge for food, as she'd sometimes found necessary with her father.

She scrambled from bed. Hard work had increased her appetite. She'd claim her place in line for hot eggs, toast, and sausage.

Once in the far kitchen, her good mood abandoned her. No one said good morning. Few acknowledged her presence with a look. Mrs. Elliott took note, of course, but she kept track of everyone.

Maddie nodded in greeting, and held out her plate to receive her portion from Miss Sullivan, then moved to the far end of a table. The others filled the chairs farthest away from her first.

She stared out the window as she ate and willed herself not to cry. Yes, they treated her badly, and expected her to endure without complaint. She did, mainly because she didn't want to give anyone the satisfaction of seeing her fail.

Some housemaids paired together as a team, but Maddie always worked alone. She hummed to fill the silence. Songs she loved, like *Oh, Susanna* and *Love's Old Sweet Song*.

Her soft voice echoed in the stillness. A lullaby and her mother's gentle smile filled her memory, and she imagined her mother singing *Birds in the Night* in harmony with her:

> *Birds in the night that softly call,*
> *Winds in the night that strangely sigh,*
> *Come to me, help me, one and all,*
> *And murmur, murmur, murmur,*

Murmur baby's lullaby.

A sob escaped. *Mama, I'm so horribly lonely.*
Don't cry, my sweet.
She knew it wasn't her mother, really, but the floodgates had opened. *I've never been this alone, literally alone, in all my life. I've been abandoned. Father didn't return for me (to my utter lack of astonishment). Not that even a small part of me entertained the notion, but the little girl in me hoped beyond hope for a rescue. Like a true father would rescue his daughter.*
You aren't alone, dearest.
Flashes of her times with Zack went through her head. She shook them away.
Zack? Who had acted as if he cared but never visited her, never asked how she was faring. If she caught a glimpse of him at a distance, he'd catch her gaze for a moment…she'd tense, waiting for a wave, or at least a smile, but he'd simply turn away. The few times he actually came inside the residence, her heart leapt. If she passed him in the foyer, she couldn't seem to find her breath, let alone her voice, but then Mr. Booth would fetch him to the library to meet with Mr. Vanderbilt. Zack followed without so much as a nod to her.
She scrubbed the tile with renewed force.
He hated her. He must. Why else would he act so cold? Of course he despised her. Why wouldn't he? She had to prove herself to him. To them all. She wasn't that scheming shrew they believed her to be. She'd set things right, no matter what any of them thought.
Even Zack.
Especially Zack.

She pushed to her feet. In passing the window, Maddie paused. On the path outside, three of the girls were on a brisk walk, their strides in perfect unison. They appeared of one goal, one mind, in complete alignment. When would she ever find such a true friend, a like-minded soul who accepted her?

Maddie Winterborn could count on one hand the number of true friends in her lifetime. Sarah, their servant's daughter, was the first, but mostly the girl had been interested in her room full of dolls and tea sets. That was in England, before Papa moved them to Spain, where Maria favored her company until Maddie's father said they must flee. Two years ago, in Jamaica, there was the boy who loved to swim and boat and just hold hands. Until Papa whisked them off to America, and their time was too brief for friends in Boston, New York, Baltimore. Now, in Asheville, the place was more beautiful, if much smaller, than the others.

But small towns had fewer people, which meant everyone here knew everyone else, and their personal business. And what they didn't know, they talked about anyway.

The odds were stacked against her. What other option did she have than to move forward?

I must endure whatever comes. I will persevere. And triumph.

Her promise would be easier to keep had Zack not utterly abandoned her.

****

The forty-minute ride to Pa's house was becoming more of a challenge. Christmas drew nearer every week, and every one of the staff scurried like rabbits running from a wolf. Who could blame them? Vanderbilt punctuated his demands with a slam of his hand on the table. The orders trickled down to Olmsted, who cracked the whip to those beneath him, including Zack.

Not enough of a reason for Zack to set aside his duty as a son. He could always get another job, but Pa was irreplaceable. These past few weeks, he'd come upon Pa a few times, stock still and eyes closed, hand clutching his left arm, a wince showing his pain. Pa denied anything was wrong, of course, but Zack had a gut feeling. A bad one. He made time to drop by every few days. A little less sleep, but he could deal with that.

Today he brought some extra potatoes Annie said she was going to throw away for no good reason, though he suspected she was merely being kind. The cook was always extra kind to him, he'd noticed.

The draft horse climbed the incline without difficulty. The quicker route to the cabin allowed him a few minutes to spare.

Dusk turned the valley shades of purple, but the sun still emblazoned the mountain peaks. The sight never failed to take away his breath. He hitched the horse and paused a moment to breathe in the forest air and take in the majesty of the mountains.

The horse scratched the dirt and threw his head. Zack brushed a hand down his neck. "I'll get you water, don't worry."

He filled the bucket at the pump and set it beneath the horse, who immediately drank half.

"Pa?" Zack leapt onto the porch, knocked once, and went inside. "You here?"

The wagon sat inside the open barn, so if not in the house, his father must be out back. *I should have chopped more wood last time.* He hated for Pa to do such hard labor, but the old man was stubborn.

He set the sack of potatoes on the table and went to the back porch. His father leaned over a stump, axe on the ground.

"Pa!" He ran to him.

"Isaac?" His father looked up at him as if he weren't sure.

"Let's get you inside. I'll make you some nice hot tea." He didn't wait for an answer but wound his father's arm around his neck and supported him. "You should let me take care of the firewood."

"I'm fine." Pa sounded grumpy.

"I know, I know." Zack helped him into the stuffed chair. "I'll get that tea. Have you eaten?"

"Earlier."

"How about some fried eggs and potatoes?" Something fast. He couldn't stay too long, but he would make certain his father had nourishment.

"Sure, son."

Zack hurriedly prepared the meal, then stoked the fire. "I'll fill the racks while you eat." He waved away an argument, and hurried to the wood pile, filled his arms with logs, and after about ten trips, his father had a good supply on the porch rack and on the smaller rack inside.

"Make sure there's no bees," Pa admonished. "Last time, a few buggers hitched a ride in on the logs."

"It's that time of year. They're drowsy."

"They're not the only ones."

After Zack fixed a mug of tea, he brought it to his father. "How are lessons?"

"Some real progress with the Ames girl. Wish I could say the same for the others."

"That bad, huh?" Zack laughed at the face Pa made.

He didn't know how his father did it, giving piano lessons to students these few years. Since he'd retired from teaching in town, though, it meant neighbors came to him. Zack wasn't the only one to visit the cabin, which was a relief. "Anything else I can do for you?"

"Yes."

Unusual. Pa never usually asked for anything. "What?"

"Play me a song." He inclined his head toward the upright piano in the corner. "You haven't played me anything in a while."

He'd barely had time for such pleasures. "I'm a little out of practice." A short one wouldn't hurt, especially if it lifted Pa's spirits. "Mr. Vanderbilt has a phonograph now. You should hear some of the records."

"I like to hear people play their instruments." He gestured to the piano, but asked, "What kind of music?"

"All kinds. John Philip Sousa and other brass bands, and some really fine singers."

His father made a noise in his throat. Zack chuckled. The same noise he himself made sometimes. The one that irritated Maddie.

He slid onto the bench and opened the cover to the keys. "Any requests?"

"How about 'Love's Old Sweet Song'?"

He stretched his fingers, began to play, and sang along:

Just a song at twilight, when the lights are low,
When the flickering shadows softly come and go,
Tho' the heart be weary, sad the day and long,
Still to us at twilight comes Love's old song,
Comes Love's old sweet song.

The lyrics conjured the image of Maddie. Sweet Maddie, who he'd dearly missed these past weeks. Such a girl would make life's struggles worthwhile. To put in a day's work and come home to her...

"Lovely," said his father. "Your ma would have liked that one. And the way you sang it. Like you truly meant it."

Zack closed the piano cover with a smile. His father was fishing for news about his personal life. "Yep, Ma would have liked that." He tossed more logs onto the fire. "I hate to leave you, but I should get back to Biltmore."

"How's the castle coming along?" Pa asked.

"Too slow for Vanderbilt's liking, but the plans expand with every meeting." He tucked a blanket around his father. "I'd rather live in a cabin in the mountains."

"You can do anything you want in this life, like I always told you."

"You did." The reason Zack had confidence in pursuing his dreams. "Anything I can do before I go?"

"Just take care of yourself." Pa threw the blanket aside and carried his dishes to the sink.

"And you better do the same. No more skipping lunch." Pa had perked up since polishing off the plate of food. Maybe he'd just needed a good meal to bolster him.

"Thanks for your help. And thank Annie for the potatoes." Pa clasped his shoulder with a wink, and then walked with him onto the porch. "Careful in the dark."

"Goliath has steady footing." And patience. Zack patted the giant neck and clambered up. "Night, Pa."

"Good night, son."

He steered the horse toward the dirt road. With the stars overhead, he'd find his way back to Biltmore, but his heart was pulled in two different directions, and both were home in different ways.

Chapter Five

Just after Thanksgiving, two new girls appeared in the morning kitchen lineup—in uniform, so both were new hires. Grace O'Malley and Nellie Keating looked about Maddie's age.

Nellie set about her work with a casual air but ran circles around Charlotte and Phoebe. She had an easy laugh to go with her easy way.

And wonder of wonders, she treated Maddie with polite kindness, and laughed off suggestions to keep her distance. "None of us are better than any other."

Grace agreed with a curt nod.

Charlotte and Phoebe seethed. Sophie, as usual, simply didn't react.

For the first time in too long, Maddie breathed a sigh of relief. "You're absolutely right. I'm the victim of poor circumstance like anyone else."

Her voice, laced with a tremor when she started speaking, by the end rose clear and strong, and so did her back. Never before had she spoken up in her own defense. Not at Biltmore to her new co-workers, and not to her father in all the years before. She couldn't have much before now, of course. She'd been too young.

But she was no longer a child. She would no longer allow others to push her to the shadows and make her invisible.

She squared her shoulders. *I am not like my father.*

"I came back to Biltmore to correct the mistakes of my father and put my own life right. I intend to do just that."

She wouldn't be silent anymore or cower in the face of a challenge. The time had come to stand up for herself.

She met each person's gaze with determination. None could hold the look for long. None except Grace and Nellie, who said, "And you will. Just like we will."

Grace gave a nod with a solemn smile. "Too right."

Nellie's smile held an air of satisfaction, and she aimed it at Maddie. "Just so."

Something bubbled up inside of Maddie, a sensation of lightness. They believed her, and believed in her. That hadn't happened in too long. Maybe since Mama had died.

She could no longer include Zack in that small group. He seemed to have forgotten she existed.

"Yes," agreed Maddie. "We all will." Together.

Before they'd finished breakfast, Mrs. Elliott swept in to address them. "As you know, Biltmore's grand opening is planned for Christmas Eve. Mr. Vanderbilt has invited many prestigious guests and expects nothing short of perfection. We will all work doubly hard to fulfill that expectation." The head housekeeper detailed how the castle would be decorated. The menu would consist of venison, chicken, partridge, broiled oysters, and an array of side dishes. Guests would begin arriving days in advance, so Biltmore must be ready. And staff should work harder than ever before.

With that, Mrs. Elliott dismissed them and left as abruptly as she had arrived.

Maddie did work harder than she ever had. But the books...the books were a siren's call. She silently begged not to be assigned to the library, but Mrs. Elliott seemed to take it as a challenge, and assigned her to roll up the rugs and scrub the floors, then polish them. Maddie did her best to concentrate on her work, but one glimpse at an intriguing title, and she was suddenly Alice, the girl in the new book she'd heard of, down the rabbit hole.

Vanderbilt had amassed a treasure trove of books. As many as twenty thousand, Maddie heard someone say. Shelves stretched along the walls, and to the ceiling, accessible by one of the spiral staircases, or by climbing a ladder that rolled alongside. A marvelous invention. If she had a house, such a ladder would definitely be the first furnishing. The books would fill the shelves, eventually.

How she'd love to have a collection like this. She lost herself reading the titles, ran her fingers across their spines. At a first edition of *Little Women*, her breath caught. How she'd wanted to read this! A family of females, with a doting (and absent) father.

She slid it off the shelf, traced the gilt-leaf engraving on the cover. Then she was in the snowy world of the March sisters, readying for Christmas…

"Miss Winterborn!"

The scolding hit her harder than a snowball in the face. Book snapped shut, she stuttered over her words, but her mind had frozen. She could produce no explanation. None that would suit.

Nor would one melt the Ice Queen who scowled at her.

"Are you a guest or a worker at Biltmore?" came the sarcastic question.

"A worker." She cast down her gaze, but the floor reflected her guilt back at her. Half still remained scuffed and dull. A testament to her daydreaming.

"Not a very good one, I fear." The woman huffed. "How dare you touch any of Mr. Vanderbilt's possessions? I daresay, you'd better not attempt to take a single volume from this room."

"I would never, I swear. I merely read a few pages. I never left the library!" Could anyone steal a story? Once read, it inhabited the reader, sparkling like a star in the dark recesses of the mind.

The arched brow raised higher. "Replace the book to its rightful spot. Then finish what you've started. You won't leave the library until this floor shines."

A curt nod. Maddie silently prayed the head housekeeper wouldn't fire her.

"I'll not tolerate another incident such as this. Understood?"

"Yes, Mrs. Elliott." Afraid to meet her gaze, Maddie curtsied.

"Then get on with it."

Another curtsy, and Maddie dropped to her knees and scrubbed, long after Mrs. Elliott had gone.

She would do her work, and think of nothing—and no one—else.

The dinner bell rang, but Maddie ignored it. For the next several hours, she worked. First scrubbing, then polishing. It was long after dark when she carried the bucket outside to empty the dirty water.

Grace followed her with her own bucket. "You missed dinner."

In the distance, lanterns on posts revealed men who swung shovels of dirt.

"I'm glad I'm not one of them," said Grace. "That's true dirty work."

"At least they'll see the fruits of their labors. Gardens, forests, ponds. Not like us, whose work is undone in a day."

"Guess that's true enough." Grace squinted in their direction. "Nice-looking fellows, eh? Weren't you friends with one?"

"The landscape engineer helped me a few times. I don't think we're friends any longer."

"Why not?"

"He hasn't visited once since I started working at Biltmore."

"Didn't you hear? His father took ill a while back."

"No, I hadn't. Are you sure?" If so, that would certainly explain his distance.

"Aye, Annie said the man travels to see his Da a few times a week, and the rest of the time, Vanderbilt has him running like mad."

"I'm sorry to hear that." And even more sorry she'd acted so selfishly. Not once had she considered Zack might have his own troubles. She should have been more understanding. And more helpful, as he would have been. She wished she could offer him support.

At the very least, she owed him an apology. If she saw him, she'd risk trying to speak with him, though she honestly hadn't caught a glimpse of him lately. He must be very busy indeed.

****

The moment Zack spied Abe, the son of Pa's neighbors the Coles, he went cold. His horse at a gallop, the boy yelled for Zack.

He dropped the shovel and waved. "Here!"

The boy pulled the mare to a dancing halt. "Ma says come quick. Your Pa's bad off. She sent my pa to fetch

Doc Jackson."

His insides twisted. "Bad off how? What happened?" Zack was already at the barn.

The boy followed on horseback. "Collapsed, Ma said. I don't know anything else."

Zack tightened the cinch on the saddle. "Guess I better find out." He swung onto the horse. "I'll be back as soon as I can," he called to whoever was nearby—he hadn't checked. Olmsted and Vanderbilt would just have to understand.

He clicked his teeth and tightened his knees. The horse took off at a run. Zack heard and saw nothing but the road ahead. Nothing would get in his way.

Goliath pushed ahead without complaint. The ride lasted an eternity, and when the cabin finally came into view, Zack patted the horse's neck. "You're the best."

At movement in the windows, he rushed inside. Doc bent over the bed, where Pa rested with his eyes closed, pale as ash. He didn't stir when Zack entered, so he moved on cat's feet to the doctor's side.

"How's he doing?"

"Could be worse." Doc straightened.

A low rumble of noise came from Zack's throat, but in his mind, his mother was in the bed, eyes closed, pale as death. And Death came for her. No matter how tight his small boy's hands squeezed, he couldn't hold her on this earth.

He'd fight harder for his father. "What can I do?"

Doc gathered his stethoscope. "Make sure he rests. No chores, no travel. Just bed rest."

"For how long?" Already, his mind was in a tumult, arranging and rearranging his days. He would make it all work.

"At least a week. After that, it'll depend on your pa." Doc clamped a hand on his shoulder. "He's got a strong will. That's in his favor."

Zack could barely nod. Was a strong will enough to keep him alive? He needed more. He needed someone to attend his needs. "I appreciate you making time for Pa today."

Doc packed away the last of his instruments. "I'll check back in a day or two. If he takes a sudden turn for the worse, you let me know."

"I will." He followed the doctor onto the porch.

Goliath snorted a reminder that Zack hadn't fetched water for him. "Sorry, boy." He filled the bucket at the pump. The horse nearly emptied it as soon as Zack set it down. He stroked the huge beast and tried to anchor his thoughts.

Pa would need him there tonight. Might as well get Goliath settled in the barn, and fed. Pa's horse would need tending, too.

He talked slow and easy to the animals, as much to calm himself as them. The world was moving fast as a shooting star, and trying to pull him along with it. He'd take things one step at a time. At the moment, it wasn't possible to figure everything out.

Hooves echoed from the road, and a horse whinnied.

Zack closed the stall and went outside.

Mrs. Ames climbed out of the wagon, and her daughter handed her a covered dish. "Thought you might be here." She handed him the dish. "How's your father?"

Time will tell. He could almost hear his father answer.

"Resting now. Doc says he should pull through, but he'll need someone to look after him." An idea struck.

"Do you know of anyone who could stay with him? A week, at least. Longer would be better."

She knit her brows. "Not right off, but I'll put word out. And I'll ask at church on Sunday."

"I'd be grateful, ma'am." The scent of the casserole awakened his appetite. "And I truly appreciate your thoughtfulness. This smells delicious."

A smile broke her concern. "I hope you and your pa enjoy it. Tell him we're all pulling for him."

"Much appreciated."

She squeezed his arm and turned for the wagon, then paused. "Until you find someone, I can sit with him tomorrow, and the next day."

An inner dam broke, and a rush of emotion almost overtook him. "Would you? I'm staying tonight, but I need to get back to work tomorrow or risk losing my job."

She nodded. "Mr. Vanderbilt needs you to finish for that grand opening he's got planned. All the town's abuzz about it."

Such a relief that she understood. "He wants Biltmore ready by Christmas Eve."

"I'm sure others will want to pitch in and help you and your pa. Don't you worry."

He watched as she steered the wagon toward home and disappeared around the bend before he went back inside.

His father slept soundly, most likely the effect of the laudanum. The casserole would have to wait till later.

After he added a few logs to the fire, Zack lit a lantern, plopped into the cushioned arm chair and stared at the ceiling. Whatever came, he'd see this through.

Don't worry. If only it was that easy.

Thank goodness for good-hearted people like Mrs. Ames.

Then Maddie popped into his mind, clear and bright as morning sun, and warmed his heart. When the time was right, he'd tell Maddie how much she meant to him. She had enough to deal with.

****

With only two weeks till Christmas, Mrs. Elliott was a blur in the hallway, and her voice grew more shrill by the hour. The entire staff worked to ready for the grand opening on Christmas Eve. Tensions grew tighter by the day.

The only two unaffected were Nellie, who rolled her eyes, and Grace. "Best to keep our heads down and steer clear."

Grace pushed back a stray strand of hair. "You'll be fine. She favors you."

"No more than you." Nellie whispered, "At least we're not *her*."

Maddie felt both their stares, and her face went hot. "Yes, be glad of that."

"I only meant…because of Mrs. Elliott. She's very hard on you."

At least they recognized it. "I don't blame her, really. I should have tried to stop my father. Convinced him to find a true job."

"At least you got to travel. See the world?"

"Hardly the world. Mostly back alleys, while my father made whatever deals he could." Shame flushed her face. "I shouldn't complain. He did what he could to keep us fed. And sometimes he couldn't even manage that much." Maddie had never told anyone such private matters. Papa would have been furious, but then, Papa had caused those embarrassing situations, hadn't he?

Grace made a sorrowful noise. "What did you do then?"

"Begged," she admitted. "Foraged in waste bins of shops and markets. Sometimes, we went hungry." More often than she liked to think about.

She'd carried the burden of shame and bitterness all those years. Too long, and all alone. A weight had lifted from her after she told the truth of her life.

Nellie tsk'd. "You poor thing."

That stopped her in her tracks. No one had ever expressed sympathy for them before. "Thank you. It's still no excuse for his behavior. I'm sure others have fallen on tough times and didn't resort to thievery."

"You kept yourselves alive." Then Nellie mumbled, "Thievery ain't the worst thing." When Maddie paused to listen, the girl went on. "My ma passed about six years ago. Pa couldn't afford to keep me, so he sent me to work. The first few positions were nightmares. People thought they could beat me, or worse. I was lucky to find a job here."

"I'm so sorry. I had no idea."

"I'm not the only one." Nellie gestured to Grace. "Grace had it just as bad, if not worse."

"Not true." Grace shook her head. "My Nana did everything she could for me, until she just couldn't anymore."

"Did you lose your parents?" asked Maddie.

Grace blew a breath. "In a way. They were heavy drinkers. Nana stepped in and took me away."

"How lovely that you shared a special bond with your grandmother." At their confused looks, Maddie blushed. "I never knew either of mine."

Grace smiled. "You're right. I guess I never thought of it that way. I was lucky."

Nellie linked arms with them both. "I think we all were, in the end."

"I'm lucky you both came to Biltmore." Her loneliness had lifted like morning mist and let sunshine burst through.

Charlotte's dark glances loomed like storm clouds. In the staff room, the girl glared with hatred when Maddie was doing nothing more than mending a seam in her dress. In the kitchen, the girl bumped her on purpose, then warned, "You'd better watch yourself, missy."

Maddie had spent years around shysters and con men. She knew when someone was up to no good. But what? It was like waiting for lightning to strike, and when it did, there'd be no escape from the electric bolt.

All she could do was watch for the moment.

It came four days before Christmas Eve, when the staff, including Mrs. Elliott, gathered for the evening meal.

Charlotte rose from her chair and stared at the table. "I hate to disrupt such an enjoyable meal, but I must speak up. A great wrong has been committed."

"Well?" Mrs. Elliott arched a brow. "Don't keep us in suspense."

"This afternoon, I saw a certain someone sneak into the library and steal a book." Charlotte spoke loud and clear, an actress reciting practiced lines, with emphasis on *sneak* and *steal*.

Electricity in the air made Maddie's skin tingle. *Here it comes.*

Mrs. Elliott grew more serious. "For heaven's sake, who?"

Charlotte lifted her chin. "Miss Winterborn. She hid it in her room."

"That's not true." Maddie wouldn't be struck down without a fight.

"Shush." For a moment, Mrs. Elliott appeared skeptical.

The heat of hatred had turned to ice. "Go and look if you don't believe me."

"Very well." Mrs. Elliott rose from her chair and gestured to Annie and Mr. Booth, who startled when she ordered, "Come with me. The rest of you wait here."

No, no! Maddie wished she could run to her room ahead of them. She knew very well what they would find. Someone had stashed a book among her things.

Annie and a more sheepish Mr. Booth followed Mrs. Elliott into the corridor and up the stairs. Minutes later, they returned.

Mrs. Elliott held up a rare volume of Shakespeare. "Would you care to explain how this came to be under your pillow, Miss Winterborn?"

"I cannot, because it was not placed there by my hand." If she had, she would have used a much better hiding place. But she knew who was to blame. "I would never do such a thing. Especially not to such a valuable book."

"Yes, you did," screeched Charlotte. "I saw you! You can't deny it."

"I never did anything of the sort." Should she accuse the girl? Or would that confirm her guilt in Mrs. Elliott's eyes?

Charlotte pointed at her, and shrieked something unintelligible.

"Get control of yourself!" Mrs. Elliott slapped the

tabletop.

In the commotion, Maddie noticed Sophie enter the room.

Sophie stepped forward. "Miss Winterborn is telling the truth. She treats books like they're gold. Only someone who didn't care about stories the way Maddie does could treat a book so carelessly." She turned to the accuser. "Either you tell them, or I will."

"I have no idea what you're talking about." Charlotte nearly spat the words.

Sophie narrowed her eyes. "I saw you place the book in Miss Winterborn's bed."

With heated tears in her eyes, Maddie pressed a hand to her chest in disbelief as much as gratitude. *Sophie! Thank you!*

Charlotte was flabbergasted. "Well, I never!"

"You most certainly did," Sophie countered.

"How could I, when I was with Phoebe all night?" Charlotte nudged her friend. "Tell them."

Phoebe's mouth worked like a chicken with no squawk, then she blurted, "Yes, that's the truth."

Maddie's heart sank. Truth was subject to interpretation, especially with these two.

Mrs. Elliott arched a brow. "Speak plainly."

"Charlotte was with me," said Phoebe.

"All night?" pressed Mrs. Elliott. "Doing what?"

"Polishing the silver," blurted Charlotte.

Annie, the cook, cocked her head. "Not in my kitchen you weren't."

"No." In the silence that stretched through the hall, the clock ticked loudly. "The small dining room." Her stance dared anyone to contradict her.

"If you were in the small dining room, how could

you have seen Miss Winterborn steal a book?"

"She…passed us by."

Sophie looked from Charlotte to Maddie and back again. "How did you know it was under her pillow?"

Phoebe huffed. "Where else would she have put it?"

"A drawer, the closet, under the bed…any number of places." Sophie seemed to consider something. "Why steal a book at all when she had easy access to the entire library?"

Charlotte gestured vaguely toward Maddie. "She's so enamored of reading, I believe she'd do anything for a book. And her father's a thief—"

Mrs. Elliott clapped hard. "Enough. I have no time for this nonsense. Guests begin arriving in a few days for the grand opening. That is what we must focus on. All of us." Her gaze swept across them all. "You are dismissed."

They began to scatter, and then Mrs. Elliott said, "Miss Winterborn."

Maddie froze. "Yes, ma'am?"

"I will consider the situation and let you know my decision." A brisk hike of her skirt, and the woman hurried off.

"Mrs. Elliott?" Maddie called after her. When she turned, Maddie said, "I should be judged on my own merits." *I am not my father*. She thought she proved that every day with her hard work.

Whether Mrs. Elliott agreed was difficult to tell. After a curt nod, she continued down the hall.

Maddie returned to her work, determined to prove herself valuable. Her hands were raw when she went to the staff room for dinner. Consumed by worry, she ate without thought. She readied for bed and, instead of reading as usual, buried herself beneath the blankets. The light winked out, and all Maddie's troubles loomed over her, monsters with snapping teeth in the night.

In the morning, Mrs. Elliott called Maddie to her office. "The situation is difficult. I'm not convinced about either your guilt or innocence. Frankly, since I took you on, there's been a string of trouble. I must leave the final decision to Mr. Vanderbilt, but I'm afraid I'm going to recommend letting you go."

"What will happen to me?" Would Mr. Vanderbilt have her arrested and thrown in debtor's prison?

"That is not up to me."

The next morning, the sight of an oversized evergreen squeezing through the front entrance brought her to a stop. A flurry of workmen carried it through the arched doorway to the main dining hall. Soon, it would stand tall and bright and beautiful.

Maddie always felt the name Winterborn suited her. Born on December 24, 1876, she grew up believing that Christmas celebrations inherently included her. Lavished with love and presents, she couldn't wait for the next one. Her mother's death changed all that. No longer a doting dad, Alfred Winterborn grew distant and bitter and shrewd. Money became his only love. So long as Maddie helped him in his schemes, she was welcome.

She wasn't sorry she'd put an end to the madness. A dishonest life was no real life at all. The trouble was, she loved her father and couldn't bear to hurt him. If only he felt the same way about her.

Less than two days until Christmas.

And tomorrow, the guests would begin to arrive.

Tomorrow was also her birthday. It might indeed be special for all the wrong reasons.

Chapter Six

Strains of piano music came through the cabin as Zack tied up Goliath. "Hope your ears don't hurt." The girl struck the keys hard, and not always the right keys. *Poor Pa.*

Propped against the pillow, his father appeared peaceful. Must have had his dose of laudanum just in time.

Zack tipped his hat to Mrs. Ames.

The woman shooed Caroline outside. "Enough piano practice for now. Mr. Kingley needs his rest."

The girl crossed the floor, dejected, so Zack said, "You play really well. Pa must be proud."

"I am." The groggy voice came from the bed. "Good work, Caroline."

Even better than a song. His father was coming back to the world. Doc Jackson was weaning him off the laudanum, which usually left Pa either asleep or in a daze.

The girl brightened, and skipped onto the porch.

Zack hung his jacket on the hook. "I can't thank you enough for all you've done, Mrs. Ames."

The neighbor beamed. "I'm doing my small part, that's all."

"Without you, and the other neighbors and church folk, we truly would have been lost."

"That's the truth," Pa croaked.

Zack had to smile. Trouble brought out the best in people, and he knew how lucky they were to have good folk who were willing to help. Together, they looked in on Pa every day. Sometimes they brought food, and Zack made an effort to do the same.

"We'd best be going." Mrs. Ames bustled about, tidying the kitchen. "There's beef stew in the dutch oven for you both." She pointed at him. "You make sure to take care of yourself, you hear? You're putting in some mighty long days."

"I'm fine." Truth was, he was a bit ragged. No matter how late his workday lasted, Zack never missed a night at his father's. He couldn't—or wouldn't—sleep a wink otherwise, up all night worrying.

Doc stopped by at least once a week. Pa was on the road to recovery, a steady but slow journey.

"Everything going all right at Biltmore?"

"Right as rain." If the rain was a deluge, that was. His workload had doubled. "We put up a forty-foot Christmas tree in the main dining hall today. Vanderbilt demands everything must be grand for the grand opening."

"That'll be some party this Christmas." She looked wistful.

He helped her with her coat. "I'm sure I'll hear about it after." He sure wouldn't be there. The help would have to plan their own celebration, on a much smaller scale. Still, the giant evergreen filled the place with a wonderful scent, not to mention the delectable smells emanating from the main kitchen.

"You'll have to tell us, then." She fitted her hat onto her head. "You two have a good night."

"And you," he called after her.

She called for her daughter and bundled a blanket around her before they started off for home.

He took a moment to breathe in the brisk evening air. The cold snap had stretched longer than a few days, and the trees and mountains had a crisp outline against the sky, a definite sign Christmas would be soon, sooner than he'd like. Work was at a hurricane pace, and not enough to show for it at the end of each day.

He was so busy getting Biltmore ready he barely had time to think about how he should be helping his father prepare for the holiday. Pa always put up a fresh tree, so Zack would find a small one. A wreath would be nice. He'd see about a fresh pie, too.

Which reminded him. A stew was ready, and he needed to feed Pa.

"Who's hungry?" he asked when he went inside.

"Just a small plate for me." His father grumbled, reaching for his spectacles, "Drat this medicine. Weakens my sight." He propped a book against his chest.

"Soon you can stop the laudanum." Not just yet. Zack spooned stew into a small bowl and set a roll beside it on the tray, which he then placed on his father's lap. "Eat up."

"Not unless you do. Where's yours?"

He should have been ravenous, but worry had twisted his stomach in knots. "I'm getting it." He made a small bowl for himself, pulled a chair beside the bed, and asked for the latest news. One thing about the neighbors—they kept his father up to date.

It did Zack good to listen to his father re-tell the tales with such animation. Another sign that Pa would triumph over his condition, even if Doc Jackson said he'd have to deal with it for the rest of his life. Lighter meals and less strenuous activity, and Pa should last a good long while.

"Enough about them." His father waved the spoon. "What about you? Things must be pretty busy at Biltmore."

"Yep, pretty busy." Zack wouldn't burden his father, though. "The gardens are really shaping up. I'll bring you out this spring. There'll be thousands of flowers blooming."

"You don't say!"

Zack went on about the statues, the conservatory, the six gardens that would surround the house. "The Italian sculpture garden will really be something. The reflecting pools are the crowning touch. And you should see the ancient medieval flags Vanderbilt hung in the dining hall. The chairs look like thrones." And always made him think of Mr. Winterborn. And Maddie. "On two walls, he hung five Flemish tapestries. They're incredible, Pa, the way they tell the myths of Venus and Vulcan." He'd love to share the story of the tapestries with Maddie. He could picture her sweet brown eyes as she listened, enraptured.

The few times he'd ventured inside Biltmore, she was nowhere to be seen. With no excuse to linger, he couldn't look for her, either. There was too much waiting to be done outside.

It could be she intended to avoid him. Who could blame her? He hadn't exactly helped roll out the welcome mat for her.

"Son?" His father watched with concern.

"Sorry." He'd let the conversation trail away. "Guess I'm tired." He scooped the last of the stew into his mouth, then the roll. "Better get the firewood before all the light's lost."

Before his father could pepper him with questions, he grabbed his jacket and gloves. "Yell if you need something."

Dark had descended when he gave up at the chopping block. He piled logs into the wheelbarrow and transferred them to the rack on the porch, then hauled several armloads in to stack near the fireplace.

Pa had dozed off, so Zack slipped the tray off the bedside table, cleaned the dishes, and left a glass of water in case his father got thirsty in the night.

The washstand provided a poor shower, but he had no energy to heat bath water. He might drown in the tub, he was so tired.

He stretched out on his old bed and willed himself to go to sleep. Instead, visions of Maddie danced through his head. Did she still think about him? Some of the men thought about her, and talked about asking her to a Christmas dance.

Word was, the other servants gave her a hard time, but that was just the routine every new employee went through, right?

He'd been holding onto the books for her. Maybe he was fooling himself, a Christmas wish for a girl who made him feel like the world was right when she was near.

He hadn't even spoken to her since she began her position at Biltmore. She likely had forgotten all about him.

He wasn't quite a Scrooge just yet, but Vanderbilt's celebration might turn him into one.

Though it was his favorite holiday, he'd be glad to see the back side of Christmas this year.

****

Waiting proved worse than torture. All morning, the additional commotion of carriages, even several automobiles, added to the rush in her head. Guests flowed in the door, languished in the library, glided up and down the stairs, and the air rang with loud chatter and laughter.

She did her best to keep her head down and work hard, but Maddie's fate hung in the balance.

At noonday, she joined the rest of the staff in the back dining hall for a hurried lunch. The great day was nearly upon them. Tomorrow was the grand opening.

Her stomach sickened when a tinkling bell sounded. Mrs. Elliott was ringing.

Mr. Booth hurried away. Moments later, he told Maddie, "She wants to see you."

Her "all right" came out as a whisper. Her brisk pace took her to outside the head housekeeper's office within moments. She straightened her uniform and knocked.

"Enter," came the reply from within.

Any hope of good news faded when Maddie saw Mrs. Elliott's expression.

Behind her stony face lurked something deeply ominous.

"I have difficult news for you." The woman had barely waited for Maddie to enter and hadn't invited her to sit.

Terminated. Police on the way. She gulped. What else could it be?

"Your father," said Mrs. Elliott, "returned to Asheville."

Maddie's mouth fell open. "Is he on his way here?" Had he remembered her birthday? Or perhaps this was a trap...

Mrs. Elliott bowed her head. "The doctor in Asheville needs to speak to you."

"I don't understand." She wanted to scream at the woman to speak the truth, plain and clear.

"Mr. Winterborn was badly beaten. That's all I know for certain." Mrs. Elliott spoke quite low, and with such seriousness.

This was worse than any trap.

The air thinned around her, and she steadied herself with a firm grip on the back of the chair. *When? Why?* "I must go to him." No one better try to stop her.

Mrs. Elliott begrudgingly nodded. "One of the men can drive you."

She could have kissed the woman. "Thank you." She ran through the kitchen to the outside. "Zack?"

He emerged from the side yard. "Maddie?"

"I need to get to Asheville right away."

He yelled to his assistant, "Will! Take over." In seconds he was at her side. "Let's go."

She hurried toward the barn.

"Wait," he called after her.

No, no, no, he can't change his mind!

He caught up to her. "First, get your coat. It's cold."

She didn't remember running back inside before climbing into the wagon already waiting outside the rear door. Without Zack beside her, solid and strong, her spirit might have withered.

Before long, they were in Asheville, at a small building with a shingle that read, "Dr. Jackson."

The office was small but clean. She only said, "I'm Madelyn Winterborn."

The doctor nodded. "This way." He led them to a tiny room in the back that might have been a closet except for the cot where her father slept.

"Father!" She whispered so as not to wake him, and held herself back so she wouldn't go to his side.

She turned to the doctor. "Will he be all right?"

"I believe he'll survive. But—" Doc Jackson said with a measure of sternness, "it will take time to recover. Unfortunately, the nearest hospital is in Charlotte. I don't recommend extended travel in his condition."

Yes, Charlotte was days away, and winter weather only complicated the matter.

"What if he stays at Pa's place?" asked Zack. "Could you look in on him?"

Doc rubbed his chin. "I suppose I could, from time to time."

Maddie took him aside. "Are you sure? Won't your father mind?"

"I'm sure he'll want to help, same as me."

"Even after everything…" She couldn't finish.

"Of course." He pressed a kiss to her forehead.

She wished she could melt into him, let her troubles melt away. But like all the others, she had to face this challenge head on. "Is it all right to move him now?"

Doc scratched his chin. "The road to your Pa's cabin is in fair shape. So long as you ride slow and keep him warm, he should be fine."

Was the doctor hazarding a guess? Or putting her father in a hazardous position? Either way, Maddie had no choice. She helped Zack bundle him up, and with her lap for a pillow, stretched him out in the back of the wagon. Every bump caused a small groan. Every mile took forever.

Zack called over his shoulder, "This last stretch gets bumpy."

She held tight to steady him. The wagon tilted up, and side to side, and finally stopped outside a log cabin.

Zack carried her father to the porch, and she held open the door. Zack passed through with her father in his arms, and she secured the latch. "Oh, hello."

Zack's father began to rise from the chair, blanket sliding to the floor.

"Please don't get up." She hurried over and helped him ease back onto the seat, then shook out the cover and placed it over his lap. "I'm so sorry to disturb you. I'm Madelyn Winterborn, by the way. A terrible way to introduce myself, barging in on you like this."

"I know who you are. And I'm happy to meet you." He may have mumbled something like, *finally,* smiling up at her.

Too many thoughts flew through her head. Had he heard the worst about them? Her face went hot. "We're so very grateful for your kindness and hospitality. My father had an awful beating."

"Yes, so I heard. We'll do what we can to help."

"We so hate to put you out. Of course, we don't expect anything else beyond a place to rest."

"Nope, you're not. Zack's old room has sat empty too long." He winked. "Believe you me, I know the power of others' helping hands. Whatever I can do, I will."

"I see where Zack gets his kind heart from." She kissed his cheek. "Thank you. Truly." She'd offer to repay him if she had anything worth offering.

His cheeks reddened, and he shooed her away but looked pleased. "Go tend your pa."

Zack stood in a doorway. "In here."

"Excuse me," she whispered and, at hearing a groan

from within, hurried to the bedside.

Her father stirred and opened his eyes.

She sat on the chair beside the bed and took his hand. "Why would you come back?"

Her father struggled to swallow. "I was…on the run. In Virginia, I think." He took a ragged breath. "I passed…the window of a pawn shop, and there it was—a snow globe just like the one your Mama gave you."

That had been so long ago. "You remembered?"

A wan smile flickered on his lips. "It was a sign. From her."

Tears welled in Maddie's eyes. She couldn't find the words to speak.

"I decided…to return to Asheville. I had to…give you the snow globe…and give you what you deserved." He met her gaze with clear eyes. "The Christmas I promised."

"Oh, Papa."

"But instead, I was beat to a pulp." He wheezed a laugh, winced, then took shallow breaths.

She fluffed the pillow behind him. "You shouldn't have come back."

"I had to. I had to give you your present." He motioned to Zack, who set a sack at his side. His hand shook as he pulled out the snow globe. "Merry Christmas, sweet girl."

"After all you went through, you saved it?" She cradled the globe with both hands. A small crack ran across the front. "It's perfect."

He turned solemn. "I had the rest of…the money. For Vanderbilt," he said to Zack.

She couldn't believe what she was hearing. "You were going to pay him back? How did you manage it?"

"Bentham." Another wince, as if the name brought back the pain of their encounter. "But he...had other ideas."

"Phineas Bentham did this to you?" She fisted her hands. "But what if they'd arrested you?"

"I couldn't...let you take the blame...for my wrongs." He tried to smile, and coughed. "Besides...nothing worked...without you."

So that was it? He wanted her to work with him again? "I'm not living like that ever again, Papa." Nor would she apologize.

"I know." He patted her hand and closed his eyes.

And yet he'd returned to Asheville? "Don't you worry. I'll take care of you." Somehow.

"I've got to get back to Biltmore," Zack said softly.

"All right." She braced for him to order her to return, too.

Instead, he gestured to the other room. "There's some food put up if you get hungry. I'll be back tonight."

He was halfway out the door when she said, "Zack..." But she couldn't express the feelings that overwhelmed her. Gratitude. Need. Fear.

He just smiled back at her. "I know. I'll see you later."

Another feeling rushed over her, a warmth that would sustain her through it all. Something like love.

****

Mr. Winterborn's story touched Zack. While they were busy talking to one another, he'd slipped the globe back into a sack. Asheville had more than its share of crafts people; surely he'd find someone to fix it.

The next night, Maddie still looked distraught. He wished he could scoop her into his arms, tell her everything would be fine. The time wasn't right for such things.

Pa rested in the chair by the fireplace. "How's he doing?"

"As well as can be expected." Zack handed his father the mug of tea he'd made. "Thanks for offering to let him stay here."

"We all do what we can for each other. Otherwise, what's the point?" Pa sipped. "Besides, she's been cleaning and cooking and looking after me, too. Can't complain about that."

Zack perched on the chair opposite, but couldn't relax. After the scare with his own father, he knew exactly what Maddie was going through.

She wandered out, and swiped her forehead with her wrist.

Zack got to his feet. "I'll make you some tea."

"That would be lovely." She wrapped a blanket around herself and stepped out onto the porch.

While he waited for the water to boil, he watched her through the window. She gazed out at the mountains as he so often did, her expression a mix of awe and contentment.

He brought the mug out to her. "Nice and hot."

She cupped her hands around it. "Absolutely breathtaking, isn't it?"

He'd always thought the Blue Ridge Mountains spectacular. "The scenery makes up for the small cabin, almost, but it's nothing like Biltmore."

"No, it isn't. It's a million times better." She looked at him. "You are so lucky."

"Lucky I found you." He hadn't meant to say it out loud. But it was true.

She hung her head and stared into the cup. "Don't say that. I only bring bad luck."

"You've gone through some hard times. Luck will turn your way. You'll see." He'd do his best to help her along that path. "Why don't you go rest?"

She studied his face a moment. "We can't thank you enough. Both of you."

"No need." Thanks was for strangers. He hoped they were closer than that.

Concern creased her brow. "I thought…"

"What?"

She gave a small smile. "Never mind. You're right, I should sleep. So should you."

He should take her in his arms. Apologize. Tell her he wanted everything to be well with her. And between them.

Instead, he opened the door for her. "I will. After I tend the animals and get in some firewood." He'd wait to open his heart to her. Right now, she needed to focus on her father.

And he had chores. Weariness set in, and he fell onto the cot after getting his father settled. Sleep erased his worries, and he awoke early and surprisingly refreshed. After stoking the fire, he took off early. Maddie had everything well in hand at the cabin, which relieved him of guilt.

At Biltmore, the others were abuzz with news. He'd just dismounted when his assistant rushed into the barn.

"Did you hear?" asked Will. "They arrested Phineas Bentham on the train."

The thief! "Did they recover the rest of money he stole from Mr. Winterborn?"

Will's wide eyes were bright. "I believe so."

"That's a relief." Vanderbilt would get back his investment. But would that ease any anger toward Winterborn?

That evening, he told Maddie about Bentham's capture.

"That's wonderful news!" Maddie beamed at him. "But, now what?"

He wanted to tell her it was over, that everything would be all right, but he just didn't know. "Mr. Vanderbilt will decide that."

"So we could still end up in prison." A small catch sounded in her voice.

"Don't give up hope. It's almost Christmas." Surely, the season's good will would put Mr. Vanderbilt in a forgiving mood.

He hadn't cheered her, though.

She stared out the window. "I worked so hard at Biltmore. I truly was beginning to think I had a future here. Now I'm not sure where I belong."

She sounded so small and insignificant. The very opposite of how Zack saw her. "Here, of course. Asheville is growing by leaps and bounds. You could both get positions here."

"Everyone at Biltmore is against me." She said it with no self-pity, just as a matter of fact.

"That's not true." He'd prove it to her.

****

Maddie couldn't bear to see his sincerity. He truly had no idea. Rather than try to explain, she shook her head. Maybe her father had the right idea. Steal away in the middle of the night and leave her troubles behind.

At her side, Zack gazed out at the mountains. "I can understand if you need to go back to England."

So it was true. Zack had no feelings for her. Still, she had no desire to return to her mother country.

"London stopped being my home long ago." Shortly after Mama died. The only family left was a cousin, long ago estranged. It would break her heart to leave. "I thought I was finally putting down roots, planting myself somewhere I could grow my life." Just like his landscape. But would take time for everything to come to fruition. That vision was fading by the day.

"You can."

His gentle urging nearly broke her heart. "Everything is all wrong." Among all the terrible birthdays, this was undoubtedly the worst.

To her astonishment, he smiled. "It's not. Believe me, in the beginning, it seems hard. But give it time. You will flourish here. You will bloom."

"You say it with such conviction, I almost believe you." But she was no flower. She had no roots.

He wiped a tear from her cheek. "I believe it. I believe in you. It's time for you to believe in yourself."

She shook her head, unwilling to fool herself into thinking she belonged in Asheville.

"What would convince you that you belong here?"

She cast about. What, indeed? What had she been looking for all along? "Personal connections, I suppose. People I love, who loved me in return." She could hardly bear to say the words. She might as well leave now, before she embarrassed herself more thoroughly, if that was possible.

He took her hands in his. "Maddie, you know how I much I care for you."

How did it feel so natural that he touch her so? Yet she found it difficult to believe. "Do I?" He hadn't exactly professed undying love. Even if he had, their situation seemed so hopeless. "But you shouldn't. You should forget me. I'm no better than an indentured servant." Freedom was years away, she suspected.

"Maddie."

The husky catch in his throat threatened to hook her, reel her in.

She backed away. "Forget me. No one else would give it a second thought if I disappeared. You shouldn't either."

His gaze sharpened, and he reached for her. "That's not—"

"Please, no." She dodged him. "I need to get back to my father." She hurried inside. How long could she hide at the cabin? Her father's health improved by the day. Vanderbilt would surely send for her soon.

****

Zack set his mind to the mission ahead and would not be deterred. To blazes with Christmas preparations. As soon as he reached Biltmore, he strode into the kitchen. "Where is he?" His commanding tone caught everyone's attention.

And everyone knew exactly who he meant.

The butler stepped forward. "In his private quarters."

"Would you please let him know I have an urgent need to speak with him?"

"I will." Mr. Booth bowed and headed for the hall.

"Thank you, Giles." If Zack no longer had a job after the meeting, he'd at least depart on good terms with the staff. Unless… "Afterward, I need to speak with the rest of you."

Their surprise was expected. Their cooperation was

not.

Mr. Booth returned. "Mr. Vanderbilt will see you."

Zack's legs turned to jelly, but he followed Giles.

Vanderbilt sat behind his large desk, moving his pen across the paper before him. "I know why you're here."

"Sir?"

The great gentleman met his gaze. "Your affection for a certain young lady has not escaped my attention. Bentham's arrest settled some of the matters, but others remain."

"I understand. Not all wrongs were made right. But justice includes mercy, doesn't it?"

"Should it?"

"I think so, yes. Miss Winterborn and her father are highly intelligent people. Hard workers, too, when given the chance, as Miss Winterborn proved by working so hard at Biltmore. And Mr. Winterborn's ingenuity holds great promise. They can contribute so much good to their futures, and to all of ours." If there was any way to open Vanderbilt's heart, it was the opportunity to do good.

Vanderbilt appeared skeptical. "You've spent time with them recently. Do you find them repentant? Willing to make such contributions?"

"I truly believe so. All they need is guidance toward the right path."

Zack couldn't believe his eyes when Vanderbilt smiled.

"I anticipated your argument." He slid the paper across the desk. "This letter clears the Winterborns of any debt toward me. If they show they can lead productive lives, I'm satisfied."

Zack was tickled pink. "You won't be sorry, Mr. Vanderbilt."

"I trust your judgment. And appreciate your hard work." Vanderbilt rose. "Please continue." He looked down his nose at Zack.

Point taken. "I'll do my best, as always." He took his leave while he could do so with dignity, and with a position to which he could return.

The day's multitude of tasks helped time pass. Dark was descending when he steered Goliath toward the cabin.

The warm yellow glow from within gave him a deeply satisfying feeling. He almost hated to break the idyllic image, but he couldn't wait to give Maddie and her father the letter.

Maddie poured hot water into four cups. "You're late tonight. I managed to save you some dinner."

The same heated feeling penetrated his insides. "Smells delicious. But first, I have something for you both. Glad to see you're up," he said to Maddie's father, who sat beside the fireplace with Zack's pa.

"My strength is returning more every day," said Winterborn. "Thanks to you. All of you."

Zack drew the envelope from his jacket pocket. "This is from Mr. Vanderbilt."

Maddie paled a little, so Zack reassured her with a grin, and inclined his head to invite her closer.

She went to his side. "What is it?"

Mr. Winterborn squinted at the writing. "My eyesight's so poor. Read it, will you, Maddie?" He handed it to her.

Her gaze flew over the contents, each line bringing more light to her face. "Oh!"

"Out loud," her father urged.

She spoke in a clear but astonished voice, then

turned to Zack. "Can it be true?"

"Mr. Vanderbilt wrote it himself."

Mr. Winterborn leaned forward. "But how? Why?"

"You have the opportunity to do real good in Asheville. Both of you." He wouldn't let on that those were his words, not Vanderbilt's.

"This feels like a dream." Maddie scanned the note again.

"Since your father's improving, I'm to bring you to Biltmore tomorrow."

"Oh." Her face fell. "For my official termination?"

"No one said as much." Zack tried not to bust out in a smile, and give away that he'd organized the meeting.

He had something to prove to her.

****

Maddie did not find Zack's good mood contagious. His urgency irritated her as they readied that morning. Even more so when he saw her irritation and it only served to elevate his mood.

So when they finally stepped inside the kitchen at Biltmore, her jagged nerves fairly tore through her skin.

Annie called, "They're here!"

Maddie fumed. An ambush? That's why Zack brought her here?

Her hard attitude softened when Sophie, Nellie, Grace, and Annie scurried in with excitement.

She whispered to Zack, "What's this?"

"Everyone who cares about you."

When she stared at him in disbelief, he reaffirmed it with a nod.

Another scan of those who surrounded her showed not an angry mob but a friendly one.

"And me, miss." Giles Booth inched beside Annie.

The cook nudged him. "Go on, tell her."

"Mrs. Elliott questioned me about the incident, and I confirmed that I saw Miss Payne and Miss Dawson in the small dining room."

Bad news, if Maddie ever heard it.

"Not polishing silver, however. They were huddled behind the door, whispering about some nonsense."

How odd. Sadly, it hadn't swayed Mrs. Elliott. "I appreciate your honesty."

"That's not all. I had to return that way, and as I did, I observed Miss Payne hurrying out of the library."

"Oh?" Maddie went still. Would that change the head housekeeper's mind?

"Miss Payne and Miss Dawson now share the pleasure of your former duties."

Maddie held a hand to her mouth to cover her smile. "Cleaning bathrooms?"

"They're lucky Mrs. Elliott didn't give them the boot."

"I wouldn't mind booting their backsides," mumbled Grace with a grin before she wrapped her arms around Maddie.

Then Nellie embraced her. "It's so good to have you back."

"Does that mean I still have a position here?" Despite having abandoned her station, and causing trouble? Did she even want to return?

From the back of the room came, "I'm afraid not."

Mrs. Elliott. Maddie braced for the worst.

The group parted to allow her entry.

"You must collect your things today," said the head housekeeper. "Biltmore requires employees who cause much less of a stir. I will, however, provide you with a decent reference."

"I'm grateful." It was more than she'd hoped for, though Maddie had no idea if it would ultimately prove useful. As far as she knew, there were no other estates in the area.

To the staff, Mrs. Elliott said, "Back to work. This is not a holiday."

Sophie came forward. "I should walk you upstairs, since you're a guest and not an employee." She grinned.

"I'd love the company." It would ease the dread of solitude while she finished the sad chore.

A look back to Zack, who waved. "I'll be outside."

She and Sophie might have been friends on an outing, the conversation was so breezy.

At the room, Maddie paused. "I'll be sorry to leave here." Biltmore had been a kind of home away from home, her first in a long time. She slid the old satchel from beneath the bed. Most of her things were already inside. Except for the book.

Her gaze flew to the night table. There it was. She pressed the volume to her chest.

Sophie said, "I hope you don't mind. I read it while you were gone. The poems really are extraordinary."

"Mama would be so pleased." She'd created another fan of Emily Dickinson. "You should petition Mrs. Elliott to allow staff to borrow from the library. Mr. Vanderbilt can't possibly read all twenty thousand books at once."

"True." Sophie gave a nod of delight. "I never thought I'd say it, but I'm going to miss you, Miss Winterborn."

"Likewise, Sophie. I don't know if I thanked you properly for speaking up, but I am so very grateful."

"I only did what was right. I'm glad I got to know you."

"I'm glad we shared this room." Maddie went to the window. The estate stretched out of sight. "Such a magnificent view. I hope the next girl appreciates it as much as I have."

"She won't be nearly as interesting as you."

When Sophie laughed, Maddie did, too. "Probably just as well. Mrs. Elliott will enjoy the peace." She hoisted her bag and turned for the stairs to hide the tear that streaked her face.

They reached the main floor, and Sophie laid a hand on her wrist. "What will you do?"

Maddie put on a brave face. "Take care of my father. After that, I don't know. Something worthwhile to make you all proud." The difficult part would be to determine what, exactly, that something was.

"We already are, Maddie."

A lump in her throat prevented her from answering the girl, so she gave a nod of gratitude.

On her way through the kitchen, Annie called, "Stop!"

Maddie's heart fell. What now?

Annie bustled over with a basket in her hands. "A little something to tide you over."

"How sweet. Thank you." The unexpected kindness overwhelmed her.

"Best of luck to you." Annie went back to chopping vegetables. "Zack hasn't gone far."

Maddie spotted him soon after she stepped outside.

He strode over and took her bag. "I'll put this in the wagon."

For a moment, she could only stand there. Like

every other day, workers swarmed around Biltmore, always adding improvements. Once finished, the estate truly would be spectacular.

She simply would not be part of it. Like everywhere else they'd traveled, Biltmore would go on as if she'd never been there at all.

Never had that bothered her before, but now it did.

She had desperately hoped to belong, finally.

Chapter Seven

The drive to the cabin brought to Zack's mind the first wagon ride with Maddie. Her silence was thoughtful this time rather than fearful. She had a lot to mull over, so he wouldn't yammer about nonsense.

Once he brought the wagon to a halt by the porch, she climbed out and carried her bag inside. As he unhitched the wagon and tended to the horses and firewood, he kept one eye on the house. Maddie moved through the rooms with purpose, yet ease. She portioned out plates for the two fathers, and sat with them at the table.

The older men had grown stronger—not yet capable of caring for themselves, but that day would come soon. Sooner than Zack would like.

The thought cast gloom over his mood. He hung up his jacket with the enthusiasm of a convicted man.

"I thought you'd forgotten your dinner." Maddie was at the stove, already preparing him a plate.

"Forgotten." That reminded him. He had. "Not dinner. Something I should have given you."

He rummaged through the case he kept in Pa's room. Beneath the spare set of clothes, he found them.

He waved away her arguments that he should eat first. "Sorry they're not wrapped." He handed her the sack first. "This was from your father. I just had someone fix the crack."

She reached inside, and recognition lit her face before she laid eyes on the globe. "I'd forgotten all about it." She ran her fingers across the smooth surface. "How wonderful. And thoughtful."

It was reward enough to see how pleased she looked. "This," he handed her the brown-wrapped package, "is from me. Merry Christmas, a little late."

"But I have nothing for you."

"I don't want anything in return. Just open it."

She tore open the paper wrapping. "Oh, my!"

"What is it?" asked her father.

"Books! Absolute treasures." She stood on tiptoe and kissed his cheek.

That. That was all he wanted. He closed his eyes and breathed in her scent.

"Do you know, Mrs. Elliott charged me with cleaning the library one day. To test me, I think. And of course, I failed." She held up *Little Women.* "Once I read the first page, I couldn't stop. And more than her reprimand, I regretted not being able to finish the story." She looked at him with such intense feeling. "You've no idea how much I love these."

"I might." He squirmed beneath her gaze. "The other was on the recommendation of the vendor, so I'll blame him if you don't like it."

She laughed. "I'm sure I'll relish every word. An adventure story!"

"So he said. You have three books now. The start of your own library."

She sighed, and turned wistful.

"What?" he asked.

"Nothing, really. It's perfect. I'll have plenty of time to read now." She set them on the counter. "Now you really must eat before it gets cold."

He followed her to the table, plate in hand. Something had turned her mood, but what? Frequent glances between scoops revealed little other than that she was upset.

Her portion was small, and she ate only half, then carried the dish to the sink. After setting the kettle on the stove, she slipped onto the porch.

He followed, and draped her coat on her shoulders. "Cold out here."

"Mm." She appeared unaffected by the weather, but deeply affected by worry.

He had to ease her mind. "Tell me what's wrong, Maddie."

"I feel rather strange."

"A lot happened today. You must be overwhelmed."

"That's not it. I'm...lost. No country. No job. No home." She abruptly faced him. "We've been such a burden on you and your father."

"No, you haven't." He thought she knew he'd welcomed her with open arms.

She twisted her fingers together. "Father isn't yet well enough to leave, but I'll search for somewhere—"

"You don't have to."

"—to stay," she went on. "After I find employment, of course. Somewhere."

"Maddie, really—"

"We won't impose on you—"

"You're not. Listen to me." He clamped his hands on her shoulders. "I'm glad you're here."

She hung her head. "You're such a good man."

"You make me want to be better." When she shook her head in confusion, his mind raced. "You won't be lost for long. You'd be a wonderful teacher. You'd be great at so many things. We could even have a farm to grow evergreens for Christmas."

"That sounds perfect. But…" She searched his face. "…'we'?"

"Yes. If you're willing. You're perfect." He flushed with embarrassment. He'd meant to say she'd be perfect for such a job. But he wouldn't take it back. With one finger, he tilted up her chin. "You are perfect."

She was so close, her warmth heated his face. The deep brown of her eyes searching his caught him up. The scent of mountain air in her chestnut hair, wild from the wind.

Her earlier kiss had left him wanting more. He brushed his lips against hers. A shot of steam pumped through his veins when she kissed him back.

"Oh god, Maddie." He couldn't hold her close enough.

Then she pulled away, astonished. "But you stayed away. I thought you hated me."

"I only kept my distance so you wouldn't get in trouble with Mrs. Elliott. And because I can hardly think straight when I'm near you. Just like Emily Dickinson's poem."

Wild Nights—Wild Nights!
Were I with thee
Wild Nights should be
Our luxury!

"That perfectly describes my feelings for you, Miss Winterborn."

She looked at him so deeply, he could have melted

as she continued with the next lines of the poem:

Futile—the Winds—
To a Heart in port—
Done with the Compass—
Done with the Chart!

"You are my heart in port," she finished.

Her words sailed into his heart and anchored there, a connection that would carry them through any storm. "And you are mine. We'll never be lost now."

"Sometimes I think I've dreamed you up, Mr. Kingley. Or wished for you so hard..." Her eyes widened. "Mr. Kingley." She said it as if for the first time.

"Yes?"

" '*A kingly love will heal your heart on Christmas.*' I thought it was my mother's deathbed fantasy. But now I understand. She meant you."

She cupped his face with her hands and gazed at him with such love, he wanted to stay like that forever.

"Your mother was a very wise woman. If my love for you heals your heart, then I'm the happiest man alive."

Behind her smile, Maddie blinked back tears. "Then you've answered my Christmas wish. This really is the best Christmas I've had in many years."

He encircled her in his embrace and held her close. "For me, too."

In the purple shadow of the Blue Ridge Mountains, he made a vow. "I'm yours alone, Maddie. Until the Appalachians crumble."

"We won't let them. We'll plant our Christmas trees

there." She wrapped her arms around his neck with a smile more beautiful than sunlight on the mountain peaks.

A word about the author...

Dog lover. Dreamer. Writer, reader, book hoarder. Multi-published in contemporary to historical, fantasy/dark fantasy to paranormal, award-winning author Cate Masters loves a good story, and sometimes mashes genres. She also writes women's fiction, fantasy and speculative fiction as C.A. Masterson. Visit her at:
https://catemasters.wixsite.com/cate-masters---c-a
or her blogs at:
http://paintingfirewithwords.blogspot.com
and
http://catemasters.blogspot.com
and in strange nooks and far-flung corners of the web.
https://catemasters.wixsite.com/cate-masters---c-a

Thank you for purchasing
this publication of The Wild Rose Press, Inc.

For questions or more information
contact us at
info@thewildrosepress.com.

The Wild Rose Press, Inc.

www.ingramcontent.com/pod-product-compliance
Lightning Source LLC
Chambersburg PA
CBHW072005170626
46813CB00005B/2027